MW01623941

SLADE'S VOW (SPECIAL FORCES: OPERATION ALPHA)

TAC-OPS SERIES

BOOK FOUR

ANNA BLAKELY

Edited by: Tracy Roelle and Theresa Huber
Proofread by: Eve Kandris, Beverley Findlay, and Amanda Zook

Dear Readers,

Welcome to the Special Forces: Operation Alpha Fan-Fiction world!

If you are new to this amazing world, in a nutshell the author wrote a story using one or more of my characters in it. Sometimes that character has a major role in the story, and other times they are only mentioned briefly. This is perfectly legal and allowable because they are going through Aces Press to publish the story.

This book is entirely the work of the author who wrote it. While I might have assisted with brainstorming and other ideas about which of my characters to use, I didn't have any part in the process or writing or editing the story.

I'm proud and excited that so many authors loved my characters enough that they wanted to write them into their own story. Thank you for supporting them, and me!

READ ON!

Xoxo

Susan Stoker

To those readers who enjoy an opposites-attract love story with excitement and danger…

This one's for you!

PROLOGUE

Marietta, Ohio

Twenty-six years ago…

"There has to be another way." Michael Stanton stared at the ranch-style home through the lenses of his TT260 night imaging monocular. "She's a mom, for Christ's sake. Her daughter's only like, what… six?"

The man on the other end of the encrypted phone call blew out an exasperated breath. "Her kid is not my problem, and she sure as hell shouldn't be yours, either," Douglas Easton shot back. "You know how this works, Michael. There's too much at stake to back out now. If you don't follow orders they'll just send someone else to clean up your mess. And if that happens, you know they won't stop with just her."

The cold-hearted prick's point was crystal fucking clear. Either Michael eliminated the person threatening to expose him for what he really was, or the people he worked for would do it for him.

They'd kill her. The kid. And when they were finished with that…

They'd kill me, too.

He sat back into his leather seat and studied the house again. Michael had known for a long damn time that this day was always a possibility. The risks of getting involved were perfectly clear, even before he chose to sell his soul to the Devil.

But the temptation was too great, his greed too strong. And when he'd gotten his first glimpse of how the other half lived, the rewards seemed to heavily outweigh the risks.

The connections. The money. The power. It was all far more than a man like him could have ever imagined. But now, because of the choices he'd made…

It's either her or me.

He'd spent a lot of time these last few weeks pondering his life choices, reflecting on that which he could have done differently. Things he probably *should* have done differently.

Both lists were long and filled with his own version of regret, but it wasn't enough for him to try to make amends. And backing out now, well…that wouldn't change a fucking thing. Nothing other than getting his ass killed, of course.

The truth was Michael loved his life. Loved the promise of the lavish lifestyle he was mere months away from securing. And dammit, he fucking *deserved* it.

He'd given up too much and worked too damn hard to lose it all now. Especially to a woman who should have had his back as he'd had hers.

Michael had tried to reason with her, too. He'd even offered to cut her in on his part of the take. But rather than seeing the opportunity for what it was, the bitch had threatened to oust him.

Only she wasn't a bitch, which was what made this so fucking hard.

Amanda Owens was kind. Brilliant. A loving wife and an incredible mother. As an agent, she was every bit as brilliant, and when the situation arose, the woman was as deadly as they came.

But she wasn't just a loving wife and mother, nor were her talents confined to playing whichever part the Agency assigned. His partner had also been the one to show him the ropes when he'd first been assigned to their unit.

Everything Michael knew about being a master spy he'd learned from her. Now, in a twist of a fate that existed solely because of one stupid, idiotic mistake, he was about to use what he'd learned against her in the most heinous of ways.

It's either her or me. Her or me. Her or me.

Over and over, the mantra rolled around inside his head as if it were stuck on a never-ending loop. The words his mind had created served as a reminder of what was at stake.

His future.

His freedom.

His *life.*

And when it came down to it, he was a selfish fucking bastard who was nowhere near ready to die.

"You're right," he told the man on the phone, cutting the car's engine with a quick turn of his wrist. "I've got this."

"You'd better. Otherwise, you know I'll have no choice but to—"

"I said I've fucking got this," Michael growled through a set of clenched teeth.

"Good." The smug asshole sounded pleased as punch. "I'm assuming you have what you need to take care of the phones, alarm system, and any externally linked cameras?"

"Jammer's already set up and ready to roll."

"Glad to hear it. The last thing we need is your ass being caught on video."

Michael glanced at the property through his monocular once more. "How sure are we that the husband isn't going to interrupt the job?"

"Very. Intel confirms Owens is at some work conference in Miami. Checked into his hotel yesterday morning, and the reservation is for the next five days. Trust me, you'll already be in the air by the time he gets the news."

He wouldn't simply be in the air; Michael would be on his way to a private beach house just outside a no-name village in Fiji. And while he laid low for a while in a place no one would think to look, Amanda's husband and daughter would be forced to lay the women they loved to rest.

Michael's gut tightened as the guilt he'd been fighting came rushing back to the surface. He'd gotten to know Rafe Owens pretty well over the last couple of years, and he seemed to be a standup guy.

According to Amanda—and the deep dive Michael had conducted while looking into the man's background—the muscular man made his living selling high-end insurance policies. Michael had laughed the first time he saw the woman's husband, convinced Amanda had been pulling his leg.

The guy looked more like he belonged in a boxing ring than behind some desk wearing a suit and tie. But Michael's suspicions had been quickly been proven wrong when the intel he uncovered corroborated everything Amanda had shared.

Rafe Owens was simply a licensed corporate insurance broker with an extreme dedication to his presumably intense workout regime. And from what Michael had witnessed while posing as one of Amanda's accounting co-workers, the other man loved his wife and child more than anything else in the entire fucking world.

Good thing he'll never know it was me.

"You still there?" The voice in the phone brought Michael back from his wandering thoughts.

"I'm here."

"Any other questions?"

"What about the little girl?"

"What about her?" The man acted as if he'd just asked about something as mundane as the weather.

"What if she wakes up?"

"It's two o'clock in the morning, and she's six. As long as you aren't a dumbass, she shouldn't hear a thing." There was a slight pause before the cold-hearted bastard added, "That being said, if she does happen to wake up, you know what has to be done."

Fuck.

Michael swallowed against the bile threatening to rush into his throat. He was a lot of things, but a child killer? No. That wasn't fucking him.

"Come on, Michael," the man spoke up again. "What's with you tonight? It's like I'm talking to the Jolly Green Giant of agents. This isn't your first rodeo, so get your head on straight and get the fucking job done."

The other man's words struck a chord. No, he wasn't green. Nowhere near it, in fact. He was an experienced operative who worked for the most clandestine agency in the world, and this wasn't anywhere close to being his first assassination.

So maybe you should get your shit together and start fucking acting like it. Otherwise…

"Anything else?" he bit out harshly, clenching his teeth together and waiting.

"Nothing other than to say good luck. And…let me know when it's done."

"Don't I always?" Michael ended the call, not waiting for a response to his rhetorical question. A second later, he broke the flip phone in two.

This situation sucked, and there were bound to be a few sleepless nights in his near future, but there was only one way this thing ended with him still upright and breathing. When it came down to it, Michael was a selfish fucking bastard to the core who put his own needs and wants above anyone else.

It didn't matter that the person he'd been ordered to kill was the closest thing to a true friend he had. Nor did Amanda's status as a wife and mother alter the path he had to follow.

The choice had been made, and the order had been given. The only thing left for him to do now was to get the job done and then get the hell out.

Michael reached a gloved hand over the leather-bound console to the weapon waiting in the passenger seat beside him. He picked up the Glock 19, and with several swift turns of his wrist, attached the long, black, metal suppressor to its barrel.

Quick. Quiet. Neat.

Those three objectives remained at the forefront of his mind as he opened the driver's door and exited the car. Michael shut it behind him with a gentle, silent push before glancing around to make sure the coast was still clear.

As expected, the farmland around him was dark and relatively still. The only movement he noted were the whispers of the wind. The only sounds were those made by creatures he had no reason to fear.

He reached into the pocket of his black, waterproof, softshell jacket and pulled out the matching ski mask he'd brought for the occasion. Michael slipped it over his head, adjusting the stretchy material into place and ensuring it covered everything except his eyes.

It was the middle of the night, and the nearest neighbor was half a mile up the two-lane road. Michael shook his covered head with a sigh at the irony of it all. He could almost hear Amanda's repeated words as she'd so often expressed her desire for a quieter life…

I don't need much, Michael. Just a modest house in the country, surrounded by rolling waves of golden fields, lush, green trees, and the quiet, soothing sounds of nature. That's the kind of life I want for my daughter. That's the life I want for my family when I get out.

His partner had said those same wistful thoughts aloud to him more times than he could remember.

And while Amanda was still planning to remain an active agent for at least two more years, she'd already started to put her long-term plans into motion, hoping to make the transition into normalcy as seamless as humanly possible.

Too bad she won't live long enough to fully enjoy what she'd worked so hard to build.

Filling his lungs with a full, cleansing breath, he let it out slowly and began the quiet trek to the ill-fated woman's home. With each of his silent steps through the trees near the field where he'd been parked, the knife sheathed at his belt brushed softly against his thigh as he moved.

The pistol in his hand felt comfortable as he kept it lowered at his side. Its weight and grip were so familiar and commonplace, that the weapon was almost like a natural extension of his arm.

For the next few minutes, Michael continued following the non-existent path, knowing it would take him to the back of Amanda's house. When prepping for the job, he'd carefully mapped out the safest, most efficient route. And as he approached the end of the tree line at the property's edge, he stopped.

Shoving the monocular into his left pocket, he squatted down next to a small pile of fallen leaves. With his free hand, Michael removed the dead foliage he'd put into place the night before to conceal the device hidden underneath.

The high-powered signal jammer weighed nearly

twenty pounds and was almost two feet in width, hence last night's trip out here. He'd use it for the job and then turn it off and walk away.

It would eventually be found, either by the cops or someone else, but Michael wasn't worried. If and when the device was found, it would merely raise more questions than answers.

He lifted each of the jammer's six directional patch panel antennas before pressing the switch on the side of the black metal base. He watched and waited until the little red light turned green. A sign that the device was working properly.

Confident the home's alarm system, cameras, and phones had been systematically blocked from use, he pushed himself back to his feet and initiated the second stage of the plan.

Michael broke through the tree line's edge, his booted footfalls silent against the evenly trimmed grass. Dressed in head-to-toe black, he blended into the shadows of the night as he made his way across his target's backyard.

He passed a swing set on his right. A wooden one with two bright blue swings, two metal rings to hang from, and one of those wavy yellow slides whose end almost touched the grass.

Thoughts of the young child it belonged to faltered his steps as he made his way past the playful structure. He could see her adorable little face so clearly in his mind. Round, dimpled cheeks. Rosy red lips. A smattering of freckles across her tiny nose. Big, blue eyes he wasn't sure she'd ever grow into, and a quick wit that was impressive for such a young age.

He hoped like hell his handler was right, and she was fast asleep in her bed. Otherwise…

No distractions, remember? Stay focused, get your ass in, and get your ass out.

With a mental shake of his head, Michael cleared his thoughts of anything that wasn't mission related. He scanned the area with a trained agent's eyes, noting how the exterior cameras' positions hadn't moved.

Previous surveillance of the property had confirmed the home's cameras and porch lights were all motioned censored. Not a single one was activated by his presence, confirmation that the signal jammer was doing its job.

The sole of his boot landed on the first step leading to the modest back deck. One by one, his legs carried him silently to the slatted platform.

To his left was an outdoor table and chair set with padded seats, their upholstery a deep red with several big yellow and white flowers. A few feet from that, near the deck's northern, wooden railing, was a smoker he wouldn't mind having for himself, and a grill that would make lovers of barbeque drool.

Michael refused to acknowledge the familiarity of the scene. He didn't think about the few times he'd spent with Amanda and Rafe on their deck, nor would he allow himself to remember watching their little girl slide down the yellow slide.

Instead, he remained on task, his attention laser focused. His only objective that of saving his own ass.

He approached the set of white French doors, double-checking that their locks were secure. With silent movements, Michael reached into the thigh pocket of his cargo pants and retrieved the special tools he'd brought with him for this reason.

A carbide tungsten alloy handled glass cutter the size of a No. 2 pencil, and a five-inch diameter black alloy glass suction cup complete with rubber handles for a steady grip.

He brought the sharp, durable blade to the glass square nearest the door's locks. Using the skills he'd learned in his first few weeks at The Farm—as they called their clandestine training facility—Michael created a circle just big enough to accommodate one of his fists.

The soft sound of the blade cutting into the glass reminded him of when he'd gone ice skating as a kid. Back when life was easy. Simple. Before he fell into the mess that had eventually brought him here.

When the circle was complete, he positioned the rounded cup in the center and squeezed its twin handles together. The move created the suction needed to secure the device's rubbered bottom to the slick surface, and with a careful but firm pull back toward him, Michael removed that portion of the glass from the door.

He bent down, placing the separated piece onto the wooden slat next to where he stood. With the push of the tiny button on the cup's base, the pressure was released, and he returned the cup and the cutting tool back to their rightful pocket.

Rising back to his full height, he slipped a gloved hand through the newly formed hole. The backs of his leather-clad knuckles cleared the sharp, rounded edge. A few short seconds later, the door was unlocked, and he was inside the house.

Phase two complete.

Slivers of moonlight led the way, their softened beams illuminating the home's quaint interior. Michael stood in the kitchen, taking precious seconds to recall the schematics of the one-level house.

Kitchen. Opened dining and living room. Hallway with three bedroom doors, one full bath, and a closet for linens.

His first steps moved slower than the racing beats of his heart. Several slow, deep breaths coupled with matching exhales brought his pulse back to a steady pace.

He could do this. He *was* doing it. And in a few short minutes, it would all be over. The threat to his future would no longer exist, and he'd be free to continue building the life he deserved.

Michael made his way through the living room

and down the nearly blackened hallway. From his previous visits here, he knew the first door he passed was the guest room. After that was a small linen closet on his left, followed by the door leading to the bathroom.

His gut tightened as he passed the last room on the right, praying the little girl behind it didn't wake up. He stopped at the end of the hall, just before entering the master bedroom. Its door was ajar just enough he was able to squeeze his body through with ease.

In the back of his mind, in a place he didn't dare acknowledge, was the fleeting thought that his target had intentionally left the door open in case her child hollered for her in the night.

Speaking of his target…

Amanda Owens lay curled up beneath the covers of her bed. Eyes closed, she was on her side, facing away from where he stood. With her pale skin and light blonde hair, the woman reminded him a lot of a porcelain doll.

She'd always been kind to him, even when she'd been handing down that fucking ultimatum. He could still hear her demanding he promise to think about the choices he'd made, and those he planned to make in the future.

Michael had fulfilled his promise, having spent that entire night thinking everything through. By morning, he'd realized Amanda was right. About him, the job…what his next steps should be.

But knowing that still wasn't enough to make him walk away. He'd gained a lot in the past several months, but he wanted more. He *needed* more. And there was only one way that would happen.

Michael approached the bed with caution, never one to underestimate the lethal government agent. He drew in a breath, lifted the gun in his hand, and pointed it at the back of Amanda's head.

The pad of his gloved trigger finger slid into the metal curve of the weapon's trigger. He squeezed, the subtle move releasing a single round of untraceable ammunition.

A soft zip of the suppressed gunshot reached his ears at the same time the bullet struck its target with perfect aim. A tuft of blonde flew up and out before falling limply around the small, circular wound.

Michael lowered the weapon back down to his side, grateful that Amanda had been asleep at the time of her unexpected death. Not only because he'd avoided confrontation, but because he could walk away knowing she hadn't suffered.

As far as deaths went, Amanda's had been peaceful and without pain. He'd known a hell of a lot of people who weren't that lucky.

Quit trying to justify this shit and get the hell out!

Michael spared his deceased partner one final

look before turning to leave. But the little girl standing just inside the doorway stopped him mid-stride.

No. No, no, no, no, no!

"Mommy?" Amanda's daughter looked at her mother's still form.

The girl's eyes were full of sleep and confusion as they slid from the bed back up to him, and all he could think about were the words he was told earlier when he was still on the phone.

If she does happen to wake up, you know what has to be done.

The man who'd helped put this plan into motion had been referring to the child Michael was staring at now. But just like when he'd heard those words the first time, everything inside him rejected the horrific notion.

I can't kill a kid. Not a fucking kid!

Not one who was innocent in every sense of the word.

He did, however, need to get the fuck out of that house. And since he was covered in head-to-toe black, and the room was mostly dark…

Michael walked toward the little girl, one slow step after another. She remained in place, the only thing moving were those big, blue eyes.

They followed him as he passed between her and the door's wooden frame. As he left the room, he was tempted to tell her he was sorry for what he had done. But he didn't dare for fear she'd recognize his voice.

A tall man dressed in black wasn't much for the police to go on. A voice, however, was another story altogether. The last thing he needed was to provide the cops with their first good lead.

Michael continued walking, refusing to look back at the little girl as he left. On his way out, he shut the kitchen door softly, and though it was silly, he reached back through the hole he'd created and reengaged the locks.

His boots hit the grass, and he took off running. He stopped long enough to cut power to the signal jammer and then resumed his hurried escape through the trees. He didn't stop until he reached his awaiting car.

Once there, he rushed to remove the stocking cap, gloves, and black jacket he'd been wearing before tossing them into a paper bag that was waiting inside his trunk. With plans to burn it the first chance he got, Michael got back into his car, started the ignition, and was back on the two-lane highway in record time.

Using one hand to steady the steering wheel, he retrieved a second burner cell from the vehicle's center console. This one was equipped with a mobile voice-distorting machine. Something he'd purposely been sure to have on hand solely for the sake of the child.

He dialed nine-one-one and listened as it rang. The operator answered, and Michael quickly gave the woman on the other end of the line Amanda's home address. His voice sounded like someone else's entirely as he relayed the pertinent information.

"The woman who lives there is dead, and her young daughter is in the house alone."

"Sir, I'm sorry. Did you say someone is dead?"

Rather than answer the question, he ended the call. They had what they needed, and the girl would be safe. As for him…

Michael used his knee to drive as he pulled the distorting device free from the phone. Once he'd tossed that back into the console's interior, he did like before and broke the cell in two halves.

He rolled down his window, tossing one half out into the night. Four miles later, he did the same with the rest. The cool, evening breeze blew through his hair, and he gave himself a few calming minutes before making the call.

"It's done," he told the man from the third and final burner phone he'd brought with him before giving it the same treatment as the others.

Final phase complete.

With his eyes on the road and his gut threatening to churn with guilt, Michael used the drive home to remind himself of the benefits Amanda Owens' death would bring. And when he laid his head on his pillow to the rising of the sun, he fell asleep with a smile spread wide across his face.

CHAPTER 1

Columbus, Ohio
Present day…

Shadow sat in the booth farthest from the door of the hole-in-the-wall diner where she waited. Moving her gaze in a casual yet constant and purposeful swivel, she kept a watchful eye on the diner's entrance, the other customers inside, and what she could see of the small parking lot through the large window on her left.

The waiting sucked. Hard. Waiting meant she had no choice but to sit alone and think. And right now, especially given where she was and why she was here, granting her mind permission to wander was some sort of next-level type of torture.

She thought about her mother—her whole reason

for upending her life to come here. She thought about her father and the note she'd left where he'd be sure to see it. The words she'd written still lingering between her every thought…

Dad,

I found the man who killed Mom. If the guys need help, call Rawlins. He knows I'm leaving town and has agreed to handle things until I get back.

Please don't try to stop me. You know this is something I have to do. Tell the team to stay safe and I'm sorry.

I love you,

~A

Shadow's heart squeezed as she thought of the team she'd abandoned to follow her quest for personal vengeance. The four-man team of highly trained, private hostage rescue specialists wasn't merely a group of voices she spoke to through her state-of-the-art satellite comms system.

Garrett Morgan, Ethan McAllister, Beckett Stone, and Slade Garrison. Those were the names of the members of Tac-Ops. Though to her, they were better known as Falcon, Apollo, Bones, and Digger.

Digger.

A different kind of hold grew tight around her heart, but she pushed it away, refusing to give it even a second's worth of conscious awareness. Regrets of any kind had no place here. Especially when what she was feeling had nothing to do with her job or this mission.

Why waste time regretting something that never had a snowball's chance in Hell of ever happening in the first place? Or fantasizing about a man who had no idea who she really was?

Why waste time, indeed?

Just because Digger's deep voice always seemed to reach her on a level no one else ever had meant diddly squat. So did the fact that, on the rare occasions his picture just happened to pop up on her computer screen, his crazy intense eyes seemed to stare straight into her soul.

Digger or Slade, it didn't matter which name she used for the sexy beast of a man. The fact was they'd never met and probably never would. And right now, her focus needed to be on her mission and nothing—or no one—else.

Period.

Shadow brushed the distracting thoughts aside just as the door to the diner was pulled open. Her lungs quickly filled with a breath of relief when she realized the man she'd been waiting for had finally arrived.

Tall and muscular, the happily married former Navy SEAL looked even more formidable in person than he did from her computer screen. Having only ever seen him on a few video calls the two had previously shared, she took advantage of the opportunity to study him closely as he casually made his way toward her.

His hair was black with a generous amount of silver strands mixed evenly within. Longer on the top and short on the sides, the salt-and-pepper locks matched the well-trimmed beard covering his chiseled jaw.

Dark, impressive tats lined the length of his arms, the permanently etched artwork adding to the silver fox's whole *stay-the-fuck-away-from-me* vibe. Shadow's focus, however, wasn't on the muscles or the hair, but rather the set of jade eyes staring back at her.

"Thanks for coming." She sent Baker Rawlins a flash of a smile as he slid into the empty bench seat across from her.

"Sounded important." The former Navy SEAL settled himself against the cushion. The burgundy vinyl upholstery creaked beneath his solid form.

"I wouldn't have called you if it wasn't." She held the tech genius's tense gaze. "You want something to eat or drink? My treat."

"Nah, I'm good. But thanks."

A symphony of conversations between the other customers filled the small diner. Shadow not only welcomed the constant humming of noise but counted on it to drown out what she and Baker needed to discuss.

"Listen, Baker…I know we don't know each other," she began. "And I get that the whole face-to-face thing isn't really your jam, but given the reason we're here, I thought it was better to be safe than sorry."

"Safe." He huffed out a sardonic breath. "Darlin', you and I both know that's a bullshit word people use so they can sleep at night."

The man wasn't wrong. The world was filled with many forms of evil, and monsters were very, very real.

"Either way, I appreciate you agreeing to meet," she told him sincerely.

"You're just lucky I was still on the mainland when you called. Though I have to say, it took me by surprise. Given who your boss is and that you work for Tac-Ops, I would have thought they'd be your first line of defense."

Guilt assaulted her as she once again thought about the team of badass operatives who often risked their lives regularly for people they didn't even know. And the way they'd gone balls to the wall when it was their soulmates' lives on the line.

Those were the jobs that stressed her out the most. Those were the missions that were often the most dangerous.

If there was one thing Shadow had learned from serving as the team's overwatch, it was that the men of Tac-Ops would do anything—risk *everything*—to protect the women they love. And this last time…

I wasn't there to help them.

"The team's had a lot on their plates lately," she muttered low.

"Ah, yes. The recent rescue involving Bones' fiancée. That was a close one, for sure. But thankfully, it all worked out in the end."

Fiancée?

A jolt of hurt sliced through her before she could school her expression. "Bones and Evie are engaged?"

It was well known amongst her and the team that their medic had been bitten hard by the love bug. But thanks to her abrupt departure, Shadow had apparently missed out on the exciting announcement.

"Sorry." Baker's brows dipped inward. "I figured you knew."

She swallowed her guilt, hating that she'd had to choose between the team and finding justice for her mother. "I knew Evie had been rescued…again." Her lips curve into a brief smile. "I just feel bad that I wasn't there to offer my support. If anything had happened to a member of the team—"

"Owens would have sent me to find you long before you reached out."

Her head dipped in a slow nod, knowing he was probably right. "Thank you, by the way. For stepping into my place to help them when I couldn't."

Like her, Baker often worked behind the scenes, using his wicked computer skills to help other special ops teams save the innocent and destroy the enemy. Most recently, he'd put those skills to use aiding Tac-Ops on their mission to save the woman who'd stolen Bones's heart.

"No thanks needed," Baker rumbled. "Although, I did tell your boss he owes me one."

Boss, father...same difference.

"I'm the one who owes you, Baker. Not Owens." Shadow sipped on the same glass of iced tea she'd been nursing for the past half-hour. "If it wasn't for your help, the guys—"

"Would have figured something else out." He shot her a knowing look.

Sighing, she asked, "When do you go back home to Hawaii?"

"Soon as I leave here."

Better get to it, girlie.

"I won't keep you, then." She leaned in, resting her elbows atop the shiny wooden table. "Were you able to find anything useful?"

He leaned to the side, the vinyl sounding off once again as he reached for something behind his back. When his hand returned, she saw that he'd retrieved a vertically folded manila folder.

"Depends on what you consider useful." He put it on the table and slid it her way. "But if a smoking gun's what you're hoping for, it's not in there. To be honest, there's not much of anything in there."

"You didn't find *anything?*" Shadow frowned as she picked up the envelope and released the thin metal clasp.

Holding it between her midsection and the table's edge, she lifted the flap and reached inside. She pulled out the thinner-than-expected stack of documents.

"The guy's clean, Shadow. As in, his ass probably squeaks when he walks."

"That's impossible. No one is that clean." She quickly scanned what she could of the first few pages, being careful not to expose the intel to anyone other than herself. "Especially a politician."

But even as those last muttered words fell softly from her lips, her heart sank, and her stomach grew heavy with a fresh dose of disappointment and dread. From what she could see of the intel Baker had brought her, he was right.

There's nothing here.

"What about his financials?" she asked as she continued to skim through the pages.

"Everything seems to be in order. The guy even pays his taxes early. Every. Fucking. Year. I'm tellin' you, Shadow…" Baker's expression was serious. "*If* something's there that we aren't seeing, whoever hid it is as good as either one of us."

"You're wrong." The ends of her long, blonde ponytail brushed against her lower back with a confident shake of her head. "Whoever covered the bastard's tracks is *better* than us."

Which meant this was going to be even harder than she thought. Shadow was admittedly one of the best hackers in the country. Baker was even better than her. But the person who'd managed to cover her target's tracks as well as they had…

"It's someone he used to work with," she whispered the words more to herself than him.

Someone within the CIA helped him cover it all up.

She hadn't shared her theory about her target being former CIA. Not with Baker or her father.

Like everything else up to this point, she had no solid proof. Accusing someone of murder was one thing. Speaking in conspiracy theories and hypotheticals about traitorous spies took it to a whole new, tin-foil-hat-wearing level.

"Listen, Shadow." Baker finally spoke up again. "Whatever's going on with this guy is none of my business. And obviously, you don't have to tell me what it is, but…I really wish you would."

"I don't want to get you any more involved than I already have," she responded honestly.

"You let me worry about me." He shot her a pointed look. "You're out here all on your own digging up who knows what kind of shitstorm, and if things start going south with this guy, you're going to need someone in your corner."

"It's…complicated."

His whiskered chin dipped low. "Complicated, I get. Complicated is something I can understand. But going down a road like *this* one… Sweetheart, this has suicide mission written all the hell over it."

"You don't even know what I'm planning, Baker."

Shadow brought her blue gaze back up to his. "And I promise you I'm not looking to die."

"Then what is it you are looking for?"

"Justice."

He held her stare a moment longer before motioning to the folder in her hands. "What did he do to you?"

"It's not about me." Shadow secured the thin flap before placing the envelope back onto the table. Keeping her voice low, she told him, "I want justice for my mother."

"You're mother?" Baker's salt-and-pepper brows dipped in the center. "What did he—"

"He killed her."

Her chest grew tight, the familiar pain making sure she never forgot. Not that she could, even if she wanted to. And she'd tried.

Silence filled their booth as she let him process the bomb she'd just dropped. Seconds later, a soft, airy whistle escaped Baker's bearded lips as he sat back against the cushion behind him.

"When? How?"

"Twenty-six years ago." She answered his questions in the order they were received. "A bullet to the back of her head while she was sleeping."

Sympathy poured from his gaze. "I'm sorry. I didn't know."

"No reason for you to know. And, before you ask your next question, let me save you the trouble. I know he's the man who killed my mother because I…" Shadow worked her throat before clearing it. "I saw him do it."

"Are you serious?" He shot back up to the table. She could see the wheels turning in his brilliant brain. "Twenty-six years ago. That means you would've been about—"

"Six." She frowned and looked away. "Yeah. I know. But it was him, Baker. I know it in my gut it was him; I just…" Her shoulders rose and fell with a deep breath and slow exhale before she met his stare again. "I need to find a way to prove it. The only way I can think to do that is to get a confession, and the only way *that* will happen is if I can figure out a way to—"

"Blackmail him into agreeing to a meeting," he finished for her.

Shadow's head dipped with a single nod. "I thought about going to the cops or the press. Telling them what I remember. Try to convince them to take me seriously. But I know how that whole scene plays out."

"What do you mean?"

"I was six, the house was dark. It was the middle of the night, and I'd just woken up. The man who shot her was wearing a mask, and *he*"—she pointed to the folder—"conveniently had a rock-solid alibi for the time of her murder. One that screams cover-up, by the way."

"Damn." He looked back at her with a mixture of

disbelief and awe. "Owens said you love a good challenge. Sounds like this one's right up your alley."

A challenge was right. She'd have to tread very, very carefully.

"I thought about going a different route," she explained. "I was going to try to get hired onto his staff, then charm my way up the ranks until I finally got close enough to the asshole to make my move. But a plan like that could take several months. Maybe longer. And by then—"

"The election will be over."

And it'll be too late.

Shadow took another sip of her tea, rolling her lips inward to keep the watered-down iced beverage from dripping onto her chin. "He makes it into the Oval Office, it'll be nearly impossible to get close to him." Her blue gaze lifted to his. "Can you understand now why this is so important to me and why this can't wait?"

He nodded. "I do. But that still doesn't change my assessment of the situation. As it stands, there's no way you're getting behind closed doors with that man. No matter what you have planned."

"I plan to kill him," she stated bluntly. "I want to stand over his bleeding body and watch the life drain from his cold-hearted eyes. But for now, I'll settle for a one-on-one."

Baker's slightly widened gaze quickly scanned the immediate area around them. "Jesus, Shadow. This isn't some dark web chat room. You can't go around saying shit like that in public."

She followed his cue and glanced around the diner. The booth behind Baker was empty. On the flip side, almost every one of the bolted swivel stools running the length of the counter to her right was occupied. But none of those people—or the two employees she could see—were paying them any mind.

Even if they were, I never said the man's name, so they'd have no idea who it is I'm planning to kill.

"Don't worry." Shadow brought her focus back to Baker. "I don't plan on giving the man a heads up."

"Let's just hope you haven't already."

The unexpected comment gave her pause. "What do you mean?"

"You said it yourself. No one's record is that clean. Given who the man is…" He let his words trail. "If you've been watching him for the past couple of weeks, there's a possibility his people have noticed you, too."

"I've been careful," she assured him.

"Going after a guy like him for murder." A quick shake of his head. "All I can say is good luck proving it."

"I don't need luck, Baker. I need something *concrete*. Leverage I can use to force his hand into a private meeting. That happens, it's all but done." *I know I can get him to talk.* "The problem is, I keep coming up against nothing but a bunch of dead ends."

The brilliant former SEAL studied her closely before a look of understanding flashed through the greens in his eyes. "That's why you want the face-to-face."

Shadow's nod was her only response.

Hell yes, she wanted a confession. One the entire world could hear. Then they'd know what kind of man he really was, rather than the wholesome family man he claimed to be.

"What's Owens' take on this?"

Baker's deep rumble brought her out of her thoughts. Clearing her throat, she pushed her shoulders back and jutted her chin.

"He's not here, is he?" One of her brows pulled to a point.

A sliver of guilt from the way she'd left things back home still pressed heavily against her shoulders. She'd carried it around for a few weeks, its weight coming and going in waves.

"Again, not my business, but the man seems to care about…your team…a lot more than the average boss. If he isn't backing you on this one-woman mission, I'm betting there's a damn good reason."

That reason is he doesn't want me dead.

"If Owens has a problem with me doing the right thing, Baker, he can fire me. Aside from that, I'm an adult. When it comes to my time away from Tac-Ops, I don't have to answer to anyone."

Because there isn't anyone outside my time with the team.

It was a truth she had no intention of sharing and a problem for another day. For now, there was only one goal in sight. Only one thing that mattered. And that was getting to the truth, once and for all.

The server brought over the check, and Shadow settled up with cash. Her generous tip for the iced tea made the older woman smile as she said, "Thank you," and walked away.

"Sorry I couldn't be more help," Baker offered sincerely. "You need anything else from me before I head out?"

The corners of her lips turned slightly upward in an appreciative smile. "No." She slid from the booth and rose to her sneakered feet. "Thanks again for coming. And…for trying." She held out her right hand and waited.

Baker stood, his large hand swallowing hers in a firm yet gentle shake. "Anytime, Shadow. And I mean that. You need anything at all—"

"Just be there for my team." Shadow released his hand and let hers fall back to her side. "Just until all this is over."

"I've got their backs, don't worry." He put her mind at ease. "But if you don't mind me asking, how long do you plan on being here?"

"As long as it takes." She held the man's green stare.

With a *fair enough* tilt of his head, Baker reminded her, "You have my number. Use it if you need it." And then, with a parting, "Stay safe out there," he turned and walked away.

She watched him go, waiting until he was out the door and walking across the lot before picking up the manilla envelope from the table and heading out herself. Shadow folded the envelope vertically in half, and then…as Baker had done…she shoved it into the back pocket of her jeans.

The hem of her black leather jacket was just long enough to keep the envelope hidden, as well as the holstered pistol she carried at her hip. She made her way down the tiled aisle between the booths and the bar stools, her head moving from side to side as she walked out into the night in search of her car.

When she'd first arrived, Shadow had purposely parked as close to the diner's entrance as she could. Even backed into the space in case the need arose for an expedient getaway.

Baker wasn't wrong to be concerned, nor was her father. But what neither man understood—what they couldn't possibly comprehend—was that until she took down the man who'd murdered her mother, Shadow would never truly be able to find peace.

I will get justice for you, Mom. Even if it's the last thing I do.

A sudden breeze lifted her ponytail into the air, whipping its thick ends around from behind her shoulder. She secured the unruly locks with her left hand while retrieving the key fob from her jacket pocket. Pointing it toward her car, parked several feet away, she pressed the button to unlock its doors.

Technically the vehicle wasn't hers. It was a rental that had been secured under a name other than her own.

Shadow opened the door and slid behind the wheel before locking herself safely inside. Her hand reached for the button to fire up the ignition, but she paused at the last minute when Baker's words from earlier rang through her mind.

Sweetheart, this has suicide mission written all the hell over it.

She shook her head with a huff, brushing off the notion that she was in any actual danger. "No one even knows you're here."

Pulling in a long, deep breath, she exhaled slowly and pushed the damn button. The car's engine came to life with a gentle roar without a single sign of impending doom or danger. With a mental reminder not to let paranoia screw with her head, Shadow put the car in gear and drove away.

The no-tell motel she'd chosen for the duration of her stay was only a few miles down the road. After the short and sweet drive there, she was grateful to find the empty parking spot directly in front of her door.

Not that she'd have had far to walk if it wasn't. The rathole, two-level establishment wasn't that big, and it had most definitely seen better days.

But it was cash only, no questions asked, and there wasn't a single camera in sight. Normally, those things would be huge ass red flags she'd avoid at all costs. In this instance, however…

No cameras plus no payment trail equals no proof I was ever here.

It was the best kind of math for someone in her situation. And since she wasn't much for sleeping these days, Shadow figured it didn't matter much where she stayed.

Right on cue, a yawn parted her lips as she opened her door and climbed out of the car. Damn. Maybe tonight would be different, and she'd finally be able to get some rest.

Feeling hopeful—and emotionally drained—she reached into her jacket pocket and pulled out the room-specific key. Stepping up onto the sidewalk lining the building's front, Shadow walked the few steps to her room.

She stopped, checking that no one had entered her room in her absence. When she saw the tiny scrap of paper was still stuck between the door's bottom right corner and the frame, she felt confident the coast was clear.

With the white plastic number plate dangling from

the metal ring, she inserted the key and gave a turn of her wrist. As expected, the door unlocked with ease.

Shadow stepped inside the unlit room, more than ready to call it a night. Tossing her room key onto the bed positioned a few feet away, she turned around and started to push the door closed when a man's hand came into view.

What the…

A set of masculine fingers wrapped around the door's edge, preventing her from closing it all the way. The reality of what was happening sank deep in an instant, and she rushed to try to slam the door shut.

A deep grunt reached her ears, and a second later, the jerk pushed against it with far more strength than she could hope to possess. Shadow lost her footing, stumbling back a few feet, but she still had the wherewithal to reach for her gun.

Her hand went to her hip. She pulled the weapon free from its holster, regaining her balance before swinging the pistol up and around.

"Don't!" The shadowed man growled, swinging an arm out to block her.

The unexpected contact caused her to lose her precious grip, and the gun went flying out of her hand.

No!

Shadow's pulse spiked with fear when her only real means of defense landed feet away, hitting the carpet with a disheartening thud. Refusing to give up, she dove forward, toward the fallen weapon.

Pain shot through both her knees as they hit the floor not far from where it lay. She reached out, her fingertips meeting with the pistol's cool metal handle. Just a little farther, and she'd be able to—

The man's warmth and weight surrounded her as his muscular form hovered over her in his efforts to grab the gun. Shadow screamed out loudly, kicking and bucking with all her might. And in one particularly satisfying move, she jammed her elbow back into the side of the face she couldn't see.

He grunted again, and for a second, she thought she might actually win. But just as the tendrils of hope began to flourish, she was flipped over onto her back with the man straddling her at her waist.

"Dammit, Shadow, stop! It's me, Digger!"

The world around her came to a screeching halt. That voice. She *knew* that voice.

I've had fantasies about that voice.

But that's all they ever were. Fantasies. Because until this very moment, she and the mouthwatering man had never actually met.

"Digger?" Shadow stared up through the moonlight with a *what in the ever-loving hell* expression. "Is that…really you?"

Slade "Digger" Garrison was the stoic leader of the Tac-Ops rescue team. He was also a man who *should* be in Charlotte, North Carolina, not—

"Yeah, princess. It's really me." The broody man sounded as grumpy as he did over the comms their team used in the field. "Now do you promise to behave yourself if I let you up, or are you gonna keep trying to shoot me?"

A rush of emotion she didn't expect blurred her already strained vision. She blinked several times, refusing to cry in front of this man, even if her tears were that of relief.

"I'm good," she managed to say, praying he hadn't heard the thickness in her voice.

But the former SEAL remained completely still, his muscular thighs and hands continuing to hold her in place. Through the touch of moonlight that had seeped in from the still-open door, she could barely make out his features…and the eyes that were laser-focused on hers.

Shadow's heart kicked hard inside her heaving chest. Minutes before she'd believed she was seconds away from death, and now…

I could stare into those eyes forever.

But rather than grabbing onto his shirt and pulling his mouth to hers—which is what she really, *really* wanted to do—she added a quipped and sassy, "You can get off of me now, Dig. Unless, of course, you plan to stay on top of me the rest of the night."

Oh, the fun we could have.

As expected, the surly Tac-Ops operative muttered an unintelligible curse before releasing her wrists and rising to his feet. Upright once again, Digger did the gentlemanly thing and offered her a hand.

Obstinate enough to refuse the help, Shadow rolled to her side and pushed herself back into a standing position. "What the hell are you doing here?" She brushed her hands down her front as a show of regained composure. "Better yet, how did you even find me?"

"The 'how' is irrelevant." The deep timbre of his voice seemed to fill the air around her. "As for the other…". Those shadowed eyes seemed to bore straight into hers. "I'm here to bring your sweet ass back home."

CHAPTER 2

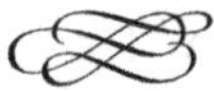

Slade watched as Shadow—fucking *Shadow*—slid past him on her way back to the room's entrance. Bypassing the door he'd forced his way through, she reached for the light switch on the wall next to its left.

A small lamp on the sorry excuse for a dresser behind him instantly came to life, casting a dim glow onto the woman who, moments earlier, had fought like hell to shoot him. She turned back around, giving him his first close-up look at the face belonging to the voice he secretly craved to hear.

Big, blue eyes. Light brown, barely arched brows. A sharp nose and cheekbones that were built for a model.

But it was the set of lips that looked as though they'd been created for the sole purpose of kissing that drew Slade in like a desperate moth to a tempting, desirable flame.

Holy. Shit.

Owens had given him the woman's picture to help in his search, and Slade had seen Shadow in person earlier when he'd been surveilling her from the diner's lot. But as he stood in her motel room, staring back at her from less than five feet away, he realized…

She's not pretty. She's fucking beautiful.

Beautiful.

Brilliant.

And stubborn as hell.

"Sorry to break it to you, big guy, but I'm not going anywhere."

The confounding woman shrugged the leather jacket from her shoulders before taking it off and tossing it onto the bed. Beneath it was a black, fitted tank top that showcased every luscious curve of her feminine form.

Toned shoulders and arms framed a perfectly curved waist. "Snatched" was the term he'd heard someone use a while back. The scooped neckline of the skin-tight top gave him the barest of peeks at her mouthwatering cleavage, and those jeans hugged her hips in a way that made him wish he could grab ahold of her and—

A purposeful clearing of her throat snapped him out of whatever momentary trance he'd just been under. Ignoring Shadow's breathtaking appearance—and the fact that he'd just been caught ogling her like a horny teenage boy—he returned his focus to the assignment he'd been given.

Find her and bring her home.

"My orders were to find you and bring you back to Charlotte, and that's exactly what I intend to do."

"Well, no offense, Dig, but your orders aren't my problem."

Dig.

She'd used the shortened version of his team nickname a hundred times before, but hearing the sexy rasp of his name from a tiny mic nestled in his ear was far different than watching it fall from her kissable lips.

"I know what you're doing," he challenged.

"You don't know anything."

Oh, princess. That's where you're wrong.

"You think Senator Stanton executed your mother nearly twenty-six years ago, and you've come to Columbus to assassinate him."

"I don't think it, Digger." Her feminine chin jutted upward with obstinance. "I *know* it was him. And while I can appreciate the fact that you're just here following Owens' orders—"

"Don't you mean your *father's* orders?" he cut her off with a more accurate truth.

The woman's tiny gasp filled the otherwise silent room.

"H-He…told you?" She stared up at him, eyes slightly widened with genuine surprise.

Slade's head dipped in a curt, confirming nod. "Right after he told me you were there the night your mother was murdered and that you'd left him a note saying you were going after the man responsible."

A flash of pain crossed over the blues of her eyes. "If you know all of that, then you understand why I have to stay."

"I get why you *want* to stay," he corrected, not blaming her one damn bit. "But you and I both know your chances of accomplishing what you've set out to do are slim to fucking none. Not to mention the danger you're putting yourself into by coming here without any sort of backup or—"

"It doesn't matter." She walked around him with purpose. "I have to at least try."

"Shadow—"

"You're right, though." She began pulling off the leather Boho-style bracelet she'd been wearing on her right wrist. "It is dangerous, so you should go."

"I'm not leaving here without you."

"Dammit, Slade…" Shadow switched to his given name as she angrily threw the bracelet on top of the dresser. "This is *my* fight, not yours."

The piece of layered jewelry missed its mark and fell over the chipped edge. The frustrated woman bent over at the waist to pick it up from the floor.

At that exact same moment, a bullet flew through the window, striking the framed mirror on the wall behind the dresser. Shards of reflective glass fell down onto the dresser with a few landing on Shadow's hunched form.

Son of a—

"Stay down!"

Slade's shouted order came as he instinctively moved in to provide cover. Another shot rang out, and splinters flew all around them as the bullet struck one of the dresser drawers to his left.

He pulled the Sig Sauer P226 Mk25 pistol from its holster at his hip while keeping his body protectively hovering above hers.

"Friends of yours?" she yelled, though her steady tone was as surprising as the woman herself.

Funny. He was about to ask her the same question.

"Don't move," Slade bit out sharply. Moving quick and low, like a rock-and-roll roadie, he hurriedly made his way over to the fractured window.

Keeping his back to the wall and his head out of the shooter's range, he used his free hand to move the very edge of the curtain slightly to the side. With a set of well-trained eyes, he scanned the area he could see.

The dark of night had fully set in, making it difficult to spot whoever the hell was trying to fill them with holes. Lucky for him, difficult wasn't the same as impossible.

There you are, asshole.

Backed in directly across the small lot was a dark SUV with no front plates. And crouched down low behind the driver's side of the vehicle's rear bumper was a man dressed in head-to-toe black.

Slade watched as the dickhead raised his pistol and prepared to shoot again.

"Stay down!" Slade shouted a second time, hoping like hell Shadow was following his orders to a fucking T.

He spun and dropped to his belly to avoid being hit, his gaze instantly sliding over to where she still lay. Relief mixed with fear when he saw her lying face-first on the floor, and he found himself praying she hadn't been hit.

She couldn't get hurt. Not on his watch. Or better yet…

Not fucking ever.

"You good?" he asked because he suddenly needed to know.

"Been better," she quipped. "You?"

His lips twitched with the urge to smile, throwing him momentarily off guard. He rarely smiled on a good day, let alone while someone was shooting at him. Only this time, the bastard wasn't shooting at him.

He's trying to kill Shadow.

An inferno of rage filled his gut as another succession of bullets began cutting through the room. Slade wanted nothing more than to jump to his feet and end this shit once and for all, but the deadly projectiles that kept coming forced him to remain in place.

Shots meant for the woman lying a few feet away struck the bed where she'd recently slept. From the corner of his eye, he saw the small eruptions of feathers and other soft materials as they exploded into the air.

He needed to get her the hell out of that room, and he needed to do it right the fuck now.

Can't go through the front…

Slade's sharpened gaze slid toward the open doorway at the back of the small room. Thanks to his earlier due diligence, he knew the bathroom had a window overlooking the narrow alley behind the motel. It was a risk for sure, but at this point, they really had no other choice.

"Bathroom window," he shouted as the gunfire continued. "Soon as this asshole stops firing, I want you to run!"

"What about you?" Shadow asked as she lifted her head just enough to meet his gaze. The concern in her eyes was touching but unnecessary.

"I'll be right behind you," he promised. "But something happens to me, you keep running until you're someplace safe."

"I'm not leaving you behind, Digger."

"Dammit, Shadow, this isn't a fucking debate. He stops shooting, I want you to keep your head down and run."

A few seconds later, the room grew eerily quiet, and he knew the time had come.

"Now!"

They both shot to their feet, keeping their bodies low as they sprinted across the room's stained carpet. With her gun in her hand, Shadow followed his orders and ran straight into the bathroom.

Another shot rang out right as Slade crossed one foot over the narrow threshold. The bullet struck the doorframe to his left, and he immediately ducked his head with a string of deep curses.

He was tempted as hell to start returning fire, but managed to hold back the retaliatory urge. The shooter needed to think that Shadow was either alone or already dead.

His already churning stomach twisted inside out at the thought. But if the son of a bitch believed he'd hit his mark and she was down, it could buy them the time they needed to escape.

Slade watched as Shadow went to the closed toilet, wasting no time putting a sneakered foot on top. With a supportive hand on the tank's porcelain lid, she quickly pushed herself up off the floor.

He stood behind her, blocking her elevated body as best he could with his. It wasn't the same as slapping a Kevlar vest on her sexy ass but, it at least offered an added buffer between her and any bullets that may still come their way.

She pushed against the window with all her might, but the painted wooden frame still refused to budge.

"It's…stuck," she grunted, her frustration more than a little clear.

Without a word, Slade stepped into the small space separating the toilet from the sink. He framed her with his uplifted arms, inadvertently bringing the front of his body flush with the back of hers.

"Move," he gave the one-word order.

Without hesitation, the sexy blonde let her hands fall back down to her sides before rotating her balanced stance enough to give him room to work. He used as much strength as he could muster to slam the heel of his free hand against the window's stubborn frame.

Again…and again…and…

There!

Layers of thick, white paint cracked and chipped as the damn thing finally broke free. Seconds later, the window was fully open, and Slade was looking outside, scanning their immediate area to confirm no additional threats.

More shots were fired from out front, but he remained focused on helping Shadow keep her balance as she began making her way through the opened window. She swung one foot outside before immediately doing the same with the other while he stayed close to the brave woman in case she started to fall.

But Shadow didn't lose her grip or tumble uncontrollably to the ground below. Instead, as if she'd made the move a thousand times before, she pushed herself free from the window and jumped.

More gunfire blasted as Slade joined his mysterious teammate in the broken and weeded back alley. The narrow strip of rough pavement separated the motel's back wall with a line of thick trees a few feet in front of where they stood.

"This way." Slade reached down and grabbed her free hand with his, ready to lead her far the hell away from any danger that might exist. His pulse quickened when she curled her fingers around his in what could only be described as a tight, trusted grip.

With him in the lead, they began running straight into the trees. He did all he could to prevent any limbs from smacking her as she followed.

If he'd been alone, there would have been no running, and he damn sure wouldn't have hid. If it were just him, he'd have stayed for what he knew would be a satisfying retribution.

But Slade wasn't alone, and the person with him was Shadow. Which meant setting aside his desire to kill for an even stronger need to protect.

Later. I'll end the bastard later. For now, all that matters is getting her someplace safe.

He continued along the invisible path through the foliage he prayed would conceal their presence. When they'd gone about thirty yards, he came to a stop, and for a moment, he simply listened.

"What are you—"

"Shhh." He held up a hand to cut her off, giving the watch on his wrist a glance as he tilted his head slightly to the side.

Though Shadow looked as though she wanted to argue, the frustrated woman clamped her mouth shut and waited. Trusting her to remain quiet until he gave the all-clear, Slade kept his focus on determining their next course of action.

According to his watch, the gunfire had stopped two minutes before, leading him to believe one of two things. Either the would-be assassin felt confident he'd hit his mark or he'd gone into Shadow's hotel room to confirm his kill.

Slade listened closely for the snapping of twigs or other signs of footfalls in the dense collection of trees. Instead, what he heard were sirens blaring to life in the distance, followed closely by the sound of tires squealing as a car quickly sped away.

"He's gone," he rumbled low to the woman still keeping a death grip on his hand.

He rather liked the feeling of her palm against his, as well as the fact that she trusted him to keep her safe. And he would, even if it was the last thing he did.

No matter what.

"What now?" Shadow's gaze found his through the thin stretch of moonlight.

"We're going to take my car and get the hell out of here before those cops you're hearing decide to stop by for a visit. We'll take the long way back to my hotel to make sure we aren't followed. I'll grab my things and then find us someplace else to crash."

"What about my things?" She looked back in the direction of the motel. "I can always buy more clothes, but my computer's still inside."

Slade barely resisted a growl but understood the woman's desire to retrieve the laptop. Computers were her life, so of course, she'd want to retrieve it. Plus, if the cops came and bagged the laptop as evidence, it could potentially lead them back to her. And *that* would open up a whole can of worms a lot of people—especially her father—needed to keep closed.

"Fine," he gave in to her request. "But we need to hurry."

"Copy that."

Shadow's on-mission response threatened another twitch of his lips. This time, however, he had no problems holding back a smile. Someone had just tried to kill her, and if she'd been alone…

They probably would have succeeded.

Forty-five minutes—and several side roads and extra turns—later, Slade was locking the door to their home for the night. It was his second hotel in less than a day, but unlike his previous one, this one was nestled in the thick of downtown Columbus.

On the plus side, the place was exceptionally rated, had a myriad of security cameras, and two off-duty Columbus P.D. officers working to keep the place safe. Truth be told, there was only one real negative he could find.

It was a big one, too. King-sized, even. Because the last available room in the place…only had one bed.

He wasn't about to share a bed with the gorgeous, spunky blonde. Not in this or any other lifetime. That, of course, left the pull-out couch. And those were always too short and uncomfortable as shit.

When the guy behind the desk had informed him of the situation, Slade had been tempted to tell him to kiss his sorry ass. But then he'd caught the expression on Shadow's gorgeous, weary face and remembered the woman had come damn close to dying less than an hour before.

This isn't about me. It's about her.

Serving as the Tac-Ops' overwatch from behind a computer screen was one thing. Getting shot at from an unknown assailant standing several yards away was another, altogether.

No matter how impressed he was by her seemingly cool and steady composure, Slade could see the turmoil hidden behind those amazing blue eyes. The woman needed food, a hot shower, and sleep. Preferably in that order.

"Wow." Shadow slid the bulging backpack from

her shoulder, gently setting it down onto a cushioned accent chair to her left. "Definite upgrade from the last place."

Her soft rasp pulled him back into the present.

"A gas station bathroom would be an upgrade from that shithole," he grumbled, walking further into the room.

"True, but a girl's gotta do what a girl's gotta do." She continued exploring the impressive space. "That place took cash and didn't ask questions, so it kept me off the grid. Until you showed up, that is." Her ponytail swung through the air as she spun back around to face him. "How did you find me, by the way?" A curious frown. "And no B.S. I want the truth."

"Oh, you want the truth?" Slade took another step toward her as feelings of betrayal sparked an unexpected rush of anger from deep inside. "That's rich coming from the woman who vanished without so much as a word to the team who counts on you to keep our asses alive while we're in the field."

Because yeah, that shit still pissed him the hell off for a slew of reasons.

"I had something I needed to take care of."

"You mean, you had someone you needed to kill."

Showing no signs of backing down, Shadow's unintimidated stare remained locked with his. "I haven't killed anyone yet, have I?" An obstinate brow arched high as she crossed her arms at her chest.

The move inadvertently pushed her full, perfect

breasts together in such a way he couldn't help but think about how perfectly they'd fit in his palms.

"I don't know what you have or haven't done because you took off on your own instead of coming to us for help," he bit back. "Jesus, Shadow. You of all people know what me and the guys are capable of. Why the hell wouldn't you come to us with this?"

"Because this is *my* fight, Slade. Not the team's. Not my father's. Mine."

His heart thumped when she used his real name for the second time that night. Over the comms, she always referred to him as Digger or Dig. Never Slade.

Truth be told, he preferred the nicknames because they reminded him of his days as a SEAL. The other name—the one his drug-addicted mother had given him the day he was born—reminded him of all the days that had come before.

Growing up dirt ass poor. Never knowing for sure when he'd get his next meal. Listening to the other kids at school talk about all the cool shit they got for their birthdays and Christmas and then going home to a run-down apartment that smelled like stale cigarettes, whiskey, and sex.

But there was something very different about the way Shadow said his name. Something he couldn't quite pin down. The only thing Slade knew for sure was that he liked it far more than he probably should.

No probably to it, dickhead. She's one of the team, remember? That means keeping your damn hands to yourself.

It also meant she had the team's support, whether she wanted it or not.

"Your fight *is* our fight, princess. I would have thought by now you'd know that."

"I'm not dragging the team into my mess, and I really wish you'd stop calling me that."

"I'll stop calling you that when you stop acting like a spoiled brat."

Pain that had nothing to do with what happened tonight clouded the fire in her eyes. "What did you just say to me?"

Shit. He hadn't meant to say that part out loud, and to be honest, he hadn't actually meant those words at all.

She wasn't acting spoiled. She was being standoffish. There was a difference, and he damn well knew it.

"Sorry. I shouldn't have said that."

"Damn right, you shouldn't have. I didn't ask you to come here, Slade. In fact, I did everything I could to keep from getting you or anyone else involved."

"Really? If that's true, then why did I see you and Baker Rawlins chatting it up inside that diner up the road from your motel?"

"How did you…" A look of understanding fell over her in an instant. "Baker. That's how you found me. He gave me up, didn't he?"

"He was worried about you," Slade told her the truth. "And given what happened tonight, I'd say he was right to be."

"Didn't give him the right to rat me out like some narc."

"Rawlins is solid, and you fucking know it, which is why he told me about your scheduled meeting when I reached out to him for help in tracking you down."

"He was worried." She scoffed.

"Yes, Shadow. He was worried. So were Owens and the team."

"And you?" Her head tilted slightly to the side. "Were you worried about me, Dig?"

She's baiting you.

"Of course, I was." Slade couldn't bring himself to lie. But then he added, "You've saved our assess time and again. I couldn't very well leave you hanging out here on your own."

Her head straightened at that last part, and he immediately knew he'd said something wrong. But whatever it was, Shadow didn't say. Instead, she walked over to her backpack and hoisted it up and over her shoulder like before.

"I'm going to take a shower." She turned away and started walking toward the open bathroom door.

His lungs emptied with a sigh. "Shadow, wait, I—"

"It's Alice, by the way."

It was Slade's turn to frown. "What?"

The confounding woman stopped shy of entering the other room and brought her pretty eyes back to his. "You keep calling me Shadow, so I'm assuming my father never told you my real name. But since you did save my ass tonight, I figure you deserve to know the truth. My name is Alice Owens, I'm thirty-two-years-old, and I'm the only child to have ever been born to Rafe and Amanda Owens. But something else you should know, and I mean this with every fiber of my being… You can take me back to Charlotte in the morning, but don't think for one second that means I'm going to stop."

She didn't wait for him to respond before disappearing into the bathroom. She shut and locked the door behind her, leaving him standing alone in the middle of the room.

Alice.

The badass computer genius who had quite literally saved his and his teammates' lives more times than he could count was named…Alice.

It was simple. Normal. So innocent and sweet.

Slade had always wondered about the fiery woman's name. He and the team had their best guesses. But not once in all the time he'd known her—albeit from afar—had he ever once considered "Alice" as a plausible contender.

What surprised him even more was just how *much* he liked it…as well as how much he liked her.

CHAPTER 3

"WE'LL BE LANDING IN ABOUT TEN MINUTES."

Shadow's attention was pulled away from the private jet's small, oval window to the man lowering himself into the empty seat at her left. Leather the color of thick, rich cream folded in beneath Digger's chiseled form.

The scent of warm, spicy teakwood and something uniquely his own swirled in the air around her. Doing her best to ignore how awesome the former SEAL smelled, she returned her attention to the endless sea of clouds.

"Okay," she responded, her tone uncaring despite the tightening in her chest. Because everything in her world was about to change.

The minute the jet's wheels made contact with the ground, there'd be no going back. Her anonymity would be shattered, and she'd be forever seen as the boss's daughter, rather than one of the team.

"I'm sorry about what happened to Evie," she said, referencing Bones' fiancée being kidnapped and nearly killed shortly after she'd vanished from the face of the earth. "I never would have gone to Columbus when I did if I'd thought she was still in danger."

"I know." His deep voice rumbled over the sound of the jet's whirling engines.

"She's okay, though, right?" Shadow turned to him, envisioning the adorable elementary teacher she'd once helped the team rescue from a cave in the Middle East. "Baker said—"

"Evie's fine." He dipped his scruff-covered chin. "Thanks to you making sure Rawlins was available for overwatch assistance after you left."

"I'd never leave you guys high and dry. I hope you know that."

"I do." Another dip. "Still don't understand why you didn't come to us for help. Especially given who and what Michael Stanton is."

She pictured the man as he looked today. Tall. Handsome. Slicked back salt and pepper hair. But then her mind became filled with the man's frozen image from that night.

Black ski mask, shirt, jacket, and pants. Black leather gloves and that big, black gun. To a six-year-old, the gun had seemed big. Especially with the suppressor attached to the barrel's tip.

It was the eyes, though. Those cold, beady eyes. That's what she remembered the most.

And it was those same eyes she'd started seeing again in her dreams a few months back. The same ones she recognized out of the blue while watching the news.

"Like I said, this isn't your fight." She turned away once more.

Several seconds of uncomfortable silence ticked by before Digger spoke up again.

"I have to ask," he started before clearing his throat. "How do you know Stanton's the one who pulled the trigger?"

Aaaand…there it was. The doubt she'd always known would come. But rather than bite off his handsome head, she kept herself cool as a cucumber, giving her shoulder a casual shrug.

"I just know."

"Come on, Shadow. You want me on your side in this, you're gonna have to give me more."

Did she, though? Want him on her side, that is. She had to admit, the thought was tempting…

You're going to have to trust someone at some point, baby girl.

"The eyes," she told him softly. "I recognized the bastard's eyes."

"His…eyes."

It wasn't a question, but more like a disbelieving statement. Which was exactly what she'd expected.

"Just forget it."

A deep roar sounded from below the belly of the jet as its landing gear began falling into place.

"Tell me," Slade prodded before adding a muttered, "Please."

One corner of her lips rose with a smirk she didn't bother trying to hide. "Please?" She brought her gaze back to his. "Wow. Layin' it on pretty thick, aren't ya, big guy?"

"I'm serious." There was no humor to be found in his sexy, dark gaze. "I'm not saying I don't believe you, so you can put that thought right out of your head. All I'm trying to do is understand…how. Not saying you're wrong." He lifted one of his strong hands as a show of defense. "Just that you were really fucking young when all that went down. And you and I both know how unreliable eyewitness accounts can be on a good day, let alone relying on a memory that's almost thirty years old."

"Look, I get it, okay?" Shadow shifted her entire body in her seat so she could fully face him. "I was a kid; it was dark, and the shooter was wearing a mask. And no, at the time, I didn't realize it was him. So I couldn't possibly make a positive I.D., right? I may have only seen his eyes, Slade, but I'm telling you… Stanton's the guy."

Speaking of eyes, his were locked on hers as if she were a puzzle he was trying to solve. Which was fair, given she knew pretty much everything there was to know about him, and he knew diddly squat about her.

"Why now?"

Aaand…this was the part of her story where she'd lose him. But since the man was like a dog with a bone…

"A few weeks ago, I was sitting at home and flipping through the channels trying to find something to watch before bed. And there he was, dressed in his fancy suit and tie with his perfect smile. He was being interviewed at some big campaign fundraising event."

Digger paused before letting his brown brows dip together in the center. "Again, not questioning your story's validity, but the guy's been in the news off and on for the past few years. First as a senator and more recently during his bid for his party's presidential nomination. But this was the first time you've seen him since—"

"I never said it was the first time," she corrected him. "You asked why now, and I'm trying to answer your question."

There was no bite there, nor had she spoken with a snarky or smartassed tone. Banter may be her usual love language, but even Shadow knew there was a time and place to let her natural smartassed self shine.

This wasn't one of those times.

"By all means…" He motioned for her to continue.

"Thank you." She flashed a quick smile. "As I was

saying, I saw him on the news and started to change the channel again, but something stopped me."

"Let me guess. It was his eyes."

"I knew there was a reason my father hired you to be Tac-Ops' team leader."

Okay, so there may have been a teeny tiny bit of sarcastic quip in her tone just then. But what was it they said about leopards changing their spots? Oh, that's right…

They don't.

The jet jostled a bit as its wheels touched back to earth, and Shadow realized she needed to hurry up with the rest of her story.

"Anyway," she continued, "I watched his entire interview with this strange gnawing in my gut. I couldn't figure out why I was so enthralled by the guy, but there was something so familiar about him. I spent the next three hours falling down the rabbit hole of Senator Stanton's life. When I began losing the fight to stay awake and learn more, I closed my computer and went to sleep." She drew in a deep breath before releasing it slowly, steeling herself for his reaction to this next part. "That night was the first time in almost twenty years that I'd dreamed about my mother. Only it wasn't a dream, Dig. It was a memory."

"It all started coming back to you."

Shadow nodded, relieved that he was starting to understand. "And just as surely as if I'd traveled through time, my mind put me right back there. I was a little girl, again, awakened by something in the dead of night. I still have no idea what, but something drew me to my parents' bedroom. And before you say it, yes, I was young, and yes, I was tired. But I saw what that masked man did. And when the shooter turned around, he looked me dead in the eyes." Her vision blurred behind a well of unshed tears. "The bastard just stood there, staring down at me like he was trying to decide something important." She swiped angrily at a fallen tear. "Then… and I remember this part so clearly…he casually strolled past me on his way out of the room, as if he hadn't just put a bullet into the back of my mother's skull."

A low curse fell from Digger's tempting lips, and he both looked and sounded pissed off on her behalf. That alone gave her a sense of comfort she hadn't realized she desperately needed.

He believes me.

"So you had this dream and then what?"

"I woke up." She smiled sadly, her throat working a painful swallow. "I went straight to my computer and pulled up Stanton's picture. That's when I knew."

The pilot maneuvered the team's private jet toward the large, open hangar to their left before bringing the giant metal bird to a complete stop. Shadow expected Digger to hop up from his seat, but he didn't. Instead, the surprising man remained in place with a solemn expression crossing over his handsomely rugged face.

"There are still a lot of questions that need to be answered."

Hope flourished for the first time in what felt like forever.

"But?" she asked, her breath freezing inside her lungs.

"I'll do whatever I can to help you uncover the truth, as long as *you* promise to accept whatever that truth is. Even if it means Michael Stanton isn't our guy."

"Oh, he's our guy, all right. I'd bet my life on it."

Those deep brown eyes seemed to reach deep as he rumbled a low, "From where I'm sitting, that's exactly what you're doing."

That may be true, but…

"You and the others risk your lives all the time in the name of justice. How is this any different?"

"That you even asked that question should tell you everything you need to know."

"Well, by all means, Dig…please enlighten me."

The muscles in his strong, chiseled jaw bulged with the clenching of his teeth as his broad shoulders and chest expanded with a slow, deep breath. And when he spoke, it sure seemed as if he were struggling to reign in his frustration.

"For starters, the guys and I don't go off on our own half-cocked without our teammates backing us up. We also don't hunt down a target without plenty of hard evidence to justify the actions we take. And unlike you, we're trained for the shit we do out in the field."

"How do you know I'm not trained?" She wasn't, of course. Not like him, anyway. But still, "Until last night, you didn't even know my first name."

"Don't need to know your name to see you're already in this way over your head. And if I hadn't shown up when I did, you and I both know we wouldn't be able to sit here and have this conversation."

He wasn't wrong, and she was more thankful for his unexpected visit to her motel room than he'd ever know. But pushing the man's buttons had always been a favorite past time, so…

"I think I held my own with you pretty well."

"Was that before or after I pinned you down on the ground? Or did you already forget about that part?"

"Oh, I remember." Shadow purposely let her gaze lower to the zipper of his jeans before bringing it back up to his overly intense stare. "I've been meaning to ask, when you were straddling my hips, was that another gun I felt in your pocket…or were you just happy to—"

"Shadow…" Her name came out all growly like a warning even as his eyes grew dark with pure male heat.

She parted her lips, fully prepared to come back with some sort of smartassed, witty quip when the jet's intercom system dinged to life, and her father's trusted pilot spoke to them from inside the cockpit.

"The engines are off, and it's safe to exit. Mr. Owens sent a car to take you both straight to Tac-Ops headquarters whenever you're ready."

"Looky there." Shadow grinned, reaching down between her feet to grab her backpack from the carpeted floor. "Guess I was saved by the bell."

Though Digger looked as though he had plenty more to say, the former SEAL held her gaze a moment longer before pushing himself to his feet. He slid out of the way, waiting not-so-patiently as she stood and followed his lead.

"We'll finish this conversation later." The surly man grabbed his own go-bag from the empty seat across from where they'd sat.

"Or not." She gave a slight shrug. "Personally, I'd much rather focus my time on finding that evidence you so badly need."

She started to walk past, toward the jet's curved exit. But the man her father had sent to bring her home apparently had other plans.

"Wait." Digger put a surprisingly gentle hand on her upper arm.

Shadow schooled her expression, unwilling to reveal just how much the simple touch truly affected her. "Yes?" She pulled the ends of her long hair free from where the strap of her bag had them trapped.

"You want justice for your mother, well guess what?" His Adam's apple bobbed with a swallow. "I want that, too. But getting yourself killed in the process won't do a damn thing but let her killer walk away."

Oh.

That was actually kind of…sweet.

"I'll meet with my father and the team, but I'm not waiting forever on this, Digger. I will get a confession from that son of a bitch, even if it's the last thing I do."

With that, she turned and made her way to the front of the plane. As she disembarked the steep metal staircase and onto the privately owned tarmac below, Shadow didn't look back to see if he was following in her steps.

She had a feeling that, for as long as she continued on her quest for justice, the tempting man would never be too far away.

SENATOR MICHAEL STANTON sat in the back seat of his government-leased Cadillac Escalade, waiting anxiously for the man he was meeting to arrive. The bullet-resistant windows were tinted a deep black, completely concealing him from the outside world.

"He's here, Senator," his driver informed him from where the other man sat behind the wheel.

James was a good man and a stellar employee. Most importantly, he was very, very good at keeping secrets.

Michael turned to his right to see the man he'd trusted with a time-sensitive task get out of his piece of shit car and walk their way. On cue, James exited the Escalade and walked around the front bumper to the other side. The back passenger door was opened, and a man Michael had known for damn near thirty years appeared outside.

"You think next time you could pick a more out-of-the-way spot to meet?" Former CIA wet work agent Douglas Easton slid onto the expensive leather, shutting the door once he was fully seated inside.

Doug had been there from the very beginning, but even he was unaware of the many skeletons hidden inside Michael's closet.

"I'm hoping there won't be a next time," Michael told him. "Of course, that all depends on what you're about to tell me. I saw on the news that a run-down motel in Columbus got shot up last night. Anything you'd like to share?"

"Not much to share, I'm afraid." The other man's expression didn't falter. "Turns out the girl got away."

The hope he'd been feeling was instantly replaced with anger. "What the fuck do you mean, she got away? You're a government assassin, for Christ's sake."

"No, I *was* a government assassin. And…I wasn't the one doing the shooting."

Anger morphed into a boiling fury, making his next words escape through a set of clenched teeth. "Tell me you're kidding."

The asshole turned to him with a pointed brow. "You know I never kid about work."

"What I know is that you said I could count on you to help clean up this mess. *You*, Douglas. Not some idiot who can't handle a simple fucking assignment."

"I've used Chuck in the past, and he's always come through. He was in the area, and most importantly, using him offered another layer of protection between you, me, and the girl you want dead."

"She's a barely-thirty, five-foot-nothing woman who, according to you, is in the city all by herself. And yet this Chuck asshole couldn't handle taking her out in that shitbag motel? And what kind of hired killer shoots up the place like it's the wild fucking west? Has he not heard of discretion for crying out loud?"

"It was a shit neighborhood where crime runs rampant. He thought making it look like a gang hit or some random drive-by would pose fewer questions than an obvious hit. And I agreed."

"So you knew his plan and just went along with it?"

"I made a judgment call in bringing him in," Doug admitted. "Clearly, that was a mistake."

"Damn right, it was a mistake. What the fuck even happened? The place looked like it had been turned into Swiss cheese. There's no way she should have been able to escape unscathed."

The other man was shaking his head before Michael even finished what he was saying.

"You know the drill. No questions, remember? If this is going to work, it's crucial that you maintain plausible—"

"Deniability," Michael cut the man off. "Yes, I know. This isn't my first rodeo, Doug."

"I'm well aware. And don't worry. Next time, I'll make sure it gets done."

"Yes, you will." He stared the former assassin down. "As soon as fucking possible."

There was a slight pause before Doug said, "So you killed the chick's mom back in the day, and you're afraid it'll come out before the election. But don't you think if she knew something, she'd have spoken up well before now? 'Cause, I gotta say, paying her off would be a whole lot easier…and less messy…than making her disappear."

"It's not money she wants."

"Then what?"

"Best guess?" Michael looked away with a loud exhale. "My head…on a silver fucking platter."

Several seconds before the other man spoke again.

"If I'm risking my ass for you, the least you could do is tell me everything you know."

"You're only risking your ass for me because you've been out of the game a while, and you miss the excitement. And because I'm paying you a shit ton of money to do it."

"And because you trust me."

"I don't trust anyone."

"You trust me a little." Doug sounded smug. "Otherwise, I wouldn't be here."

Michael looked back at the man and smirked. "I suppose you're right." After pulling in a deep inhale, he let the air out slowly. "I'm pretty sure she also knows I was with the Agency."

"How the hell does her daughter know you were CIA?"

"I don't know for sure that she does."

Another brief pause ensued and then, "Okay, now I'm really confused. I assumed the Owens woman's desire to see you dead had to do with her suspicions that you were somehow connected to her mother's death. But if there's a chance she doesn't even know you were an agent, then why would she think that you—"

"She saw me, Doug." Michael cut the man's question short with a truth he hadn't uttered to another soul in nearly three decades. "I never told you, but… the night I broke into their house, and I shot my partner in the back of the head…Alice Owens saw me do it."

A low whistle filled the air as Doug ran a hand over his five-o-clock shadow. "You've got to be kidding me."

"I wish I was. But now do you understand the importance of making this go away?"

"I do." His former colleague nodded. "Don't worry. I'll find her, and when I do, she won't have the chance to get away."

CHAPTER 4

SLADE OPENED THE DOOR TO HIS BOSS'S OFFICE AND waited to the side as Shadow stepped into the private space. He followed her in, shutting the door behind him.

"Glad to see you both made it back in one piece," Rafe Owens' English accent was thick as he stepped out from behind his large mahogany desk.

The former British Intelligence operative walked over to where Slade stood, and the two men shook hands.

"For a minute, there, I wasn't sure that was going to happen." Slade shifted his stare to the woman on his right. Sensing the thick tension between father and daughter, he felt compelled to let the man know, "She handled herself pretty well, all things considered."

"She never should have been there in the first place."

The man was in his mid-fifties, but aside from the generous amount of gray hair mixed with brown, and a few etched lines in his seasoned, face, you'd never know it. Owens was tall, built like a brick shithouse, and still as capable of taking out the bad guys as any other man on their team.

"Uh…hello…" Shadow waved a hand in the air. "*She* is standing right here."

Trust me, princess. I know exactly where you are.

And though she didn't know it yet, Slade had no intentions of letting her out of his sight again.

Owens turned his attention to his daughter, though he didn't move in any closer. "From what I understand, you're only here because Mr. Garrison was lucky enough to have arrived at your motel room in the nick of time."

"I would have gotten myself out if he hadn't."

"Perhaps." Owens nodded. "Lucky for you, you didn't have to find out."

"This time."

The woman's under-the-breath comment pissed Slade off far more than it should have.

"There won't be a next time," Slade informed her briskly.

Shadow's blue eyes turned his way, her mesmerizing stare filled with overt curiosity. "No?" She gave a slight tilt of her head. "And what makes you think that?"

"Because I'm going to make damn sure that doesn't happen."

Their gazes remained locked for several intense seconds, and he tried like hell to figure out what she was thinking. But then the infuriating woman blinked it away, and just like that, it was gone.

"Careful, big guy." Shadow gave a slight click of her tongue. "You shouldn't go around making promises you can't keep."

Oh, I intend to keep it, all right. Whether you like it or not.

But before he could tell her that, Owens decided to step back in.

"Sweetheart, I understand that you're used to taking care of yourself, and normally I'm prone to fully agree." His boss seamlessly shifted from Tac-Ops owner to father. "But since you chose to start this war, I have no choice but to take control of the situation."

Shadow eyed the powerful man with suspicion. "What does that mean, you're taking control?"

"As of this moment, I'm assigning Slade as your personal bodyguard for the foreseeable future."

"I don't need a—"

"You were damn near shot to bloody hell less than twenty-four hours ago," Owens came close to losing his carefully controlled temper. "So yes, you do need a bodyguard, and I can think of no one else more capable than this man right here."

Slade's chest tightened at the sentiment. As far as atta boys went, that was a pretty damn good one.

Especially considering they were talking about protecting the man's only daughter.

"I take it I don't have a say in the matter?"

"You lost your say when you chose to go off half-cocked after a man you had no business pursuing."

"Pursuing?" Shadow snorted. "You make it sound like I was trying to date the guy."

"I know exactly what you were trying to do." Owens retorted. "And that little plan of yours was going to do nothing but wind up getting you killed."

"He shot her dead while she was sleeping, Dad. Don't you want him to pay for taking her away from us?"

"Of course, I do. And if your memories from that night are to be trusted, then I promise you, the man *will* pay."

"Memories are all I have left," she reminded him. "And you're right. Someone did try to kill me last night. Which, by the way, wouldn't have happened if I weren't on the right track."

The woman did have a point.

Feeling compelled to back up her assumption, Slade told his boss, "She's right. Stanton must have recognized her at some point and got spooked." He glanced back over at Shadow with a shrug. "It's the only thing that makes sense."

"I was careful," she rebutted. "I never let myself get too close or—"

"Doesn't matter." He cut her off. "Either he or

one of his protection detail had to have noticed you watching him. And if you think your memories from that night are clear, I'm willing to bet his are, too."

"I was six, Digger."

"Again, it doesn't matter. A man kills someone—especially someone who had, at one time, been close to him—they aren't likely to forget the only eyewitness to the crime. Six or Sixty, I'd bet you've never been far from Stanton's mind. And with him in the running for the most powerful political position in the world…"

"He isn't about to let you ruin his chances at the White House." Owens picked up right where his trailing words left off. "Which is why you must have round-the-clock protection until we can figure out a way to bring the bastard down. In the meantime—"

"Mr. Owens?" Their office manager's voice came through the landline on the man's desk. "The rest of the team is here, and they're all waiting in the conference room."

"Thank you, Ashley," his boss responded in kind. "Please tell them we'll be in shortly."

"Yes, sir." A soft click let them know the well-vetted woman had ended the call.

Uncertainty stole the spark from her previously challenging demeanor, and before he could keep from it, Slade heard himself saying, "It's going to be okay."

Shadow looked over at him, her search for assurance obvious in those vibrant blue eyes he could get lost in forever. "Do they know I'm here?"

"Not yet," Owens answered for him. "All I told them was that I needed them to come to the office as soon as possible."

"They're going to be pissed." She gave a nervous lick of her lips.

"I doubt it," Slade offered his opinion. "They're just going to be glad you're still upright and breathing."

Owens quickly backed him up. "He's right. The team was worried sick about you while you were gone. As was I."

"I'm sorry," Shadow apologized to her father for the first time since they'd arrived. "I shouldn't have left the way I did."

"No. You shouldn't have," his boss agreed. "But what's done is done, and there's no erasing the past. The only thing we can do now is move forward, and I think the best place to start is for you to finally meet the rest of your team."

Her gaze slid back to Slade's as if she needed him to confirm what her father had just said. With a single dip of his chin, he let her know she was going to be okay.

"All right, then." She blew out a breath and headed for the door. "The sooner we get this over with the sooner we can start discussing the next steps in our plan."

Owens watched as his daughter opened the door before sliding his gaze to Slade's. The two men shared a look that spoke volumes, each silently vowing to do whatever it took to make sure Shadow remained safe.

But as he followed her out of the office and down the hallway toward the Tac-Ops conference room, his gut filled with a sense of impending doom unlike any he'd felt before. Not for the conversation that was minutes away from transpiring, but rather for the danger that very well may follow.

Someone in Senator Stanton's close circle not only knew Shadow's true identity, but they also wanted the too-smart-for-her-own-good woman permanently silenced. And since she clearly had no plans of backing down from this war she'd already started, Slade and the others would need to be on high alert until a winner was finally declared.

And if he'd learned anything in his dealings with politicians over the years, it was that they'd do just about anything to ensure they didn't lose.

Shadow stopped outside the conference room door, her shoulders rising and falling with a deep, steadying breath. Without thinking, Slade placed a gentle hand against her lower back, the ends of her long, blonde waves tickling his skin.

"Nothing to be scared of, princess." He spoke quietly in her ear. "Just go in there and tell them your story. Trust me, these guys are going to understand."

Appreciation shone in the blues of her incredible stare before she reached for the knob and opened the door. Slade followed her into where his teammates awaited, the murmurs of conversations between the others halting the second they walked into the room.

Owens addressed the team as a whole on his way to his place at the front of the table. "I'd like to introduce you to Alic. Or, as you like to call her… Shadow."

* * *

SHADOW'S HEART thumped nervously as the three men sitting around the large, oval table stared back at her with matching *holy shit* expressions. It was like one of those dreams where you were caught standing in front of a group of people wearing nothing more than your underwear and a smile.

This would be the part where you say hi.

"H-Hi." She suddenly wanted to crawl in a hole and hide. But since that wasn't an option… "It's nice to finally meet you all in person."

"You're Shadow?" The man she recognized as Beckett "Bones" Stone arched his brows up high. "As in…*our* Shadow?"

Unlike what she'd expected, the handsome medic didn't look mad or upset by her presence. With the plan to pull him aside later to apologize for her absence during his fiancée's harrowing rescue, Shadow focused on the here and now.

"That's me." She smiled. "Last I checked, anyway."

"Oh, yeah." Garrett "Falcon" Morgan grinned with a nod of his head. "I'd recognize that voice anywhere.

"Well, hot damn!" Bones shot up from his chair and marched her way. "It's so good to finally meet you in 3D."

Before Shadow knew what was happening, she felt herself being wrapped up tight in the former Marine's arms. A tiny squeal escaped the back of her throat when she was hoisted up off her feet in the biggest bear hug she'd ever received.

"Good to meet you, too, Bones." She hugged him back. Despite her plan to tell him later, she heard herself whispering, "I'm so sorry I wasn't here to help with—"

"It's all good." He didn't even let her finish. "Evie's okay, and you're back, so as far as I'm concerned, all is right in the Tac-Ops world."

Tears stung the corners of her eyes, but she blinked them away. Next, she came face-to-face with Falcon, and another tight hug ensued.

"Come here, you." The man who served as Tac-Ops' top sniper pulled her into his muscular arms. "Damn, girl. I never thought this day would come."

"Me, eeither." Ethan "Apollo" McAllister was next in line. The dark-haired former SEAL surprised her when he, too, brought her in for a friendly embrace. "I thought we got called in for another job."

"You did." Her father's deep response brought an end to the celebration.

Apollo released his hold and took a step back, his almost black eyes sliding to the man standing to Shadow's left.

"Must be a big one to bring our girl to us in person."

"It is," their boss confirmed. "And I brought Shadow in to meet you all because she *is* the job."

"Boss?" Bones frowned, his confusion obvious to her and everyone else in the room.

When her dad shot her an uncharacteristically hesitant glance, Shadow took it upon herself to explain.

"Why don't you boys have a seat while I tell you a little story?"

"Storytime, huh?" Falcon smirked as he returned to his chair. "This should be interesting.

Interesting.

That was one way to put it.

"Shadow, I can—"

"It's okay." She cut her father's offer short. "I've got this."

Shadow waited for the men to sit before she began. Standing a few inches back and to her right, Digger remained in place with no obvious signs of moving.

Suit yourself, big guy.

After a quick clearing of her throat, she decided

to dive right in. "I'm sure the intricate details will come later, but for now, I'll save you all some time and give you the short and sweet version."

And that's exactly what she did. Over the course of the next few minutes, Shadow went through the bullet points of her life up to this point.

Witnessing her mother's murder. *Check.* Growing up never knowing the killer's identity or motive. *Check.* Her recent dream and the revelation that had followed. *Check. Check.*

And when she shared her deep seated suspicion that Senator Stanton was the man she believed to have shot her mother in cold blood, several under-the-breath curses created a dull rumble throughout the entire room.

"There's something Shadow isn't saying." Her father regained control of the group as he glanced over at her with a guarded smile. "It's a secret that's been kept for reasons that will be obvious by the time we're finished here today. But since I trust you all with her life, I suppose now is as good a time as any to tell you the full truth. And that truth is, this woman isn't merely your team's overwatch or my employee." He cleared his throat before looking back over the team and telling them, "Her name is Alice Owens, and she's… my daughter."

The room grew silent. It was as if the world's volume had been turned off as Shadow stood between her father and Digger. She waited with bated breath for the team's response, and when it came, it was pretty much exactly what she'd envisioned.

"Shadow's your…daughter?" Falcon's eyes grew even wider than they had when she'd first been introduced.

Apollo's dark gaze bounced between her and his boss as he ran a hand over the dark scruff covering his jaw. "Wow. I did *not* see that one coming."

"Me, either." Bones shook his head in surprise. "All this time. I mean, it's your business, of course, but why keep it a secret?"

Shadow took it upon herself to answer, purposely letting her next words trail. "Murdered mother, former MI6 father… I'm guessing you boys are smart enough to understand the need to keep my existence a secret from, well, everyone."

"Everyone?" Falcon frowned. "Who's everyone?"

"Uh…pretty much the entire world," she informed him.

"After her mother's murder, I moved us from Ohio to Charlotte," her father explained. "Anyone doing even a deep dive into me will find exactly what I want them to find. A man who worked his way up to the top of the insurance ladder, eventually opening what is known to the world as Travel Assurance Coverage Operations." A name given to correspond with the team's actual Tac-Ops nomenclature. "The leader in private travel insurance, as well as the other private policies you are all very familiar with."

"But underneath, as you also know, is the truth," Shadow jumped back in. "That the insurance company is a front for your team, making it possible for you to do what you do without media attention or political backlash."

"Don't you mean what *we* do?" Bones shot her a knowing glance. "You're as much a part of this team as we are, darlin'. Don't ever forget that."

Warmth spread within her chest, and damn if she wasn't fighting back another unexpected rush of tears. Lucky for her, her father regained control of the conversation, wrapping up the remaining pertinent facts.

"What Shadow is saying is that I chose to keep the fact that I have a daughter a secret because I felt the need to protect her from both the man who killed her mother and those who might wish her harm as a way of getting back at me."

"How?" Apollo asked. "Wouldn't a quick search show you once had a kid?"

"It would," Shadow once again answered for her father. "It would also reveal that same child's death a couple of years later."

A deep growl sounded from behind her, drawing her attention to the man responsible. Her breath caught when she met Digger's cold, hard stare. He looked angry, though she wasn't sure why.

The poor man's been shot at, forced to sleep on an uncom-

fortable hotel room pull-out, and now he's been assigned as your twenty-four-hour babysitter. It's no wonder he's mad.

But there was something more in his dark brown gaze. It was a protector's glare, and though the man looked far from happy, his expression—and mere presence—instantly made her feel safe.

"Between my father's contacts within MI6 and the alphabet agencies"—she continued—"as well as my knowledge of computers and awesome hacking skills, we all but erased any trace of my existence after the age of eight."

"Okay, I have to ask…" Bones sat up a bit straighter. "How'd you fake die?"

Another disapproving sound reached her ears, but Shadow ignored the surly team leader's displeasure and answered the other man's question. "Accidental drowning."

Simple. Believable. And they had the falsified documentation to prove it.

Apollo's broad shoulders huffed with a breathy chuckle. "Was there a funeral?"

"On paper, yes." She nodded. "I even have my very own headstone in a small cemetery across town."

She'd gone there once, a couple of years ago. The day had been rainy, the sky gray with a thick layer of clouds.

For obvious reasons, most people avoided visiting the cemetery in the rain. Which was precisely why she'd gone there that day. Less chance of being seen.

Shadow wasn't sure what she'd expected to feel, seeing her name etched in the small stone like that. Truth be told, it was all very surreal.

"What about where you live?" Falcon asked next. "I'm assuming there's a mortgage or lease with someone's name that isn't yours."

"The lease to my apartment is under a well-vetted alias, as are my cell phone, bank account, and the few credit cards I own. I paid for my car in cash, so that's a non-issue, and according to the IRS, I'm an independent contractor who does computer troubleshooting for several companies that don't actually exist."

"Damn." Apollo dipped his chin with approval. "Sounds like you've covered all your bases and then some."

"That's what we thought, too," her father chimed back in. "But then my headstrong daughter got the idea to traipse off on a solo path of vengeance, and while she was busy stalking Senator Stanton in Columbus, her cover was blown."

"Blown?" Falcon looked to her, then Digger, before returning his attention to the man who signed their paychecks. "You sure?"

"Someone shot up her motel room last night," Digger finally spoke for the first time since coming into the room. "So yeah. We're pretty damn sure."

"You were shot at?" Bones immediately looked

her up and down as if checking for possible injuries. "Shit, are you okay?"

"I'm fine." Shadow gave Digger a sideways glance. "We went out the back, through the bathroom window, and into some trees. The shooter took off, and we got the hell out of there."

"We?" Bones eyed them both closely before locking his gaze on Digger's. "You were there, too? In Shadow's hotel room?"

"He was there because he was ordered to find Shadow and bring her back home before she could get hurt," her father answered. "Thankfully, he did."

"I'm confused." Apollo's dark brows dipped inward. "How were you recognized if everyone thinks you're dead?"

"That's the million-dollar question." Shadow met the man's curious stare. "I was careful, left no money trail, used a burner phone when needed…" She sighed. "The truth is, I have no idea how anyone could have possibly figured out my true identity."

But they had, and apparently, they were not at all pleased that she was still alive.

"Something else you should know about Senator Stanton." Her father looked first at her, and then at the others. "He wasn't simply a lawyer like it says on his lengthy and impressive resume. He's former CIA."

What the…

"You knew?" Shadow stared up at her father, surprised by his unexpected revelation. "I mean, I suspected, given his too-spotless record, as well as the manner in which Mom was killed. But I never could find any proof."

"And you won't." He shook his salt-and-pepper head. "Someone did a damn good job at covering up his past, and the only people capable of accomplishing something that involved is the Agency. But to answer your question, yes. I knew. Just like I knew your mother was an agent, as well."

A round of shockwaves filled her system as she processed the bomb her father had just dropped. "*Mom* was CIA?"

Her mother's involvement in the secretive agency made surprising sense, and yet, it left Shadow with even more questions than before. If she'd been working as a government spy, it could explain why someone had wanted her dead.

An enemy she and her team had been chasing could have decided to kill rather than be killed. Or perhaps someone connected to an op from her mother's past tracked her down as a means of revenge.

The eyes Shadow had seen behind the mask that night hadn't belonged to some unknown assailant. And since Stanton was the one who pulled that trigger…

"Mom knew too much." Shadow looked back at her father. "She had to have seen something she shouldn't have. Something Stanton thought was worth killing for in order to keep it quiet. Either that or she was working with—"

"Your mother wasn't dirty." Her father seemed to read her mind, the mere thought shooting a fiery anger into his eyes. "She was one of the best, most loyal agents the CIA has ever had. Of that, I am utterly certain."

Despite the sharp bite of his words, the conviction in her father's tone gave Shadow a sense of relief and comfort. So she gave him a slight nod, letting him know she believed everything he'd just said.

"What happens next?" Bones looked to her for the answer.

But it was her father who responded with a plan of his own making.

"Once we're done here, Digger will take Shadow to a secured location, where they will remain until the threat to my daughter has been eliminated."

Shadow's heart dropped, and her anger rose. "Excuse me?" She swung her widened gaze in her father's direction. "No. I am *not* going into hiding while that murdering asshole roams around scot-free."

"You started a war, my dear." His expression was as serious as she'd ever seen it. "And I can promise you that man's desire to see you *truly* dead is every bit as strong as your need for revenge."

"He's right," Digger rumbled low. "Stanton has more to lose now than ever before. If he was the one behind last night's shooting, then he's already shown he'll do whatever it takes to make sure you're stopped. Now, I didn't get a good look at the shooter, but I'm pretty damn confident Stanton wasn't the one pulling the trigger. That means, there's at least one man still out there willing to do his dirty work for him, and as of right now, you're—"

"His number one target," Shadow finished for the man who'd saved her life once already. "I'm not scared of Michael Stanton, Digger."

She would have thought that was already abundantly clear.

But those brown eyes of his locked tightly with hers as he rumbled a deep, "You should be."

The look on his handsomely rugged face sent shivers down her spine. Digger was one of the toughest, most capable men she knew. He'd proven himself countless times with his team, as well as last night, when he'd risked his own life to save hers.

And now, unless she could find a way to turn the tables back on Stanton, he may very well have to do it again.

CHAPTER 5

Tac-Ops safe house

Later that evening…

"I can't believe my father owns this place."

Slade entered the last of the security system's six-digit code before turning and facing the woman standing in the cabin's modest entrance. "You didn't know?"

"Nope." Shadow shook her head while letting her beautiful gaze soak in the rustic scenery. "I had no idea this cabin even existed. Of course, up until a few hours ago, I also didn't know my mom was a government spy, so there's that."

He bent down and picked up the bags they'd packed for their stay and carried them farther into the open space. Their first stop after leaving the office was at a big-box store so Shadow could get enough clothes and toiletries to last her several days. After that, they'd made a quick run by his apartment so he could grab a few extra things, as well.

"I knew it was here," Slade commented on the cabin. "But this is the first time I've ever been."

He had to admit, the two-story structure was the nicest safe house he'd ever seen. With its exposed log walls, wooden floors, and windows that stretched damn near to the ceiling, it looked more like a hunter's resort than a place to hide out from a killer.

"The master bedroom is over there." Slade pointed to the doorway on their left. "But you and I will be sleeping upstairs."

With her backpack slung over the same shoulder she'd recently shrugged, Shadow turned back around to face him.

"You and I?" A playful look flashed behind her stunning gaze. "I'm flattered, big guy, but don't you think you should at least take me out to dinner first?"

His heart thumped and his dick twitched at the mere idea of the two of them sharing the same bed. And though he knew her comment had been made in jest, there was something other than quipped humor hiding deep within the woman's sarcastic demeanor.

She's as tempted by the notion as I am.

"There are two bedrooms on the second floor."

His jaw muscles twitched with the clenching of his teeth. "I'll take the one closest to the stairs."

That way, if danger did somehow manage to find them, it would be his ass on the front lines. Not hers.

All signs of humor left her playful expression as she told him, "In case I haven't said it yet, I'm sorry."

"Why?"

"Why am I sorry?" A soft huff of a breath fell from the half-smile lifting one corner of her luscious lips. "Oh, let me count the ways. Let's see, I'm sorry for going MIA on the team and not coming to you guys instead. I'm sorry I'm the reason you were shot at last night…and for almost shooting you myself. And I'm sorry because now, because of me, you're stuck pulling babysitting duty in the middle of nowhere for however long my father decides."

"That sounds like a lot."

"Yeah, well…" A small shrug. "Apparently, so am I."

The woman *was* a handful. A fact that had been made clear from the very start. But Shadow was also intelligent, capable, and determined to right a wrong from her past.

Even he couldn't fault her for that.

"You already apologized for your little disappearing act," Slade told her. "And yeah, you should have come to us first. But I understand why you did what you did."

"You do?"

He gave a quick nod of his head. "You went to Ohio to get justice for your mom while also trying to protect the team and your father by keeping us out of the loop. Not saying it was the right call, but…I get it."

"Thank you."

"There's something else you need to accept, though." Slade stared back at her with laser focus. "You have to know that what happened to your mother wasn't your fault."

Shadow frowned, her lids blinking quickly as she gave her head a quick shake. "I never said it was my fault."

"Didn't have to. The guilt you feel is written all over your gorgeous face."

He hadn't meant to call her gorgeous while discussing her mother's murder, but the compliment had slipped out as though it was the most natural thing for him to say. Luckily, the conflicted woman either hadn't caught it or was choosing to ignore it altogether.

"I was a kid when she was shot, Digger." Her tone thickened with defense. "It's not like I could have done anything to stop a grown man with a gun."

"You're right." He took a slow step toward her. "You also had no way of knowing it was Stanton behind that mask."

"I *should* have known." She set her backpack down onto the log, dining room table to her left. "I'd met him before that night. Once, when my parents invited him over for dinner."

"So you met the guy one time when you were six years old, and you think that means you should have known it was him? Come on, Shadow. You're a hell of a lot smarter than that."

The two stood there, staring at one another as though they'd reached an impasse. Nothing he said would ease the misguided guilt the woman felt, and she'd never be able to convince him she was a fault for anything other than possessing a daughter's undying love.

Was it a smart choice to go running after a killer by herself? Absolutely not. Did he understand why she'd felt the need to do so? Yes. He did. But what he needed to make sure she knew…what he was certain she didn't fully understand was that—

"You're not alone in this, you know?" Slade held her gaze as he gave the solemn vow. "The team and I…your father…we're going to figure this all out. I just need you to promise not to do anything reckless in the meantime."

"Me? Reckless?" She shot him a sideways smirk. "Never."

"I'm serious, Shadow. You might know computers, but I know killers. And one who's willing to send a guy to shoot up a fucking motel room just to take you out isn't someone we should underestimate. Shit goes sideways again, I need to know you'll do like you did at the motel. You do what I say when I say it. No questions, no arguments."

"In spite of recent events, I've never been very good at following orders." The gorgeous blonde shrugged. "Just ask my father."

"Your father isn't here, princess. I am." He took another step toward her.

He was standing so close to her now, Shadow had to tilt her head back to keep looking him in the eyes.

"Why do you call me that?" she asked with what appeared to be genuine curiosity. "Do you think I'm a spoiled brat? Because I can assure, that's not even close to the tr—"

"Your bed."

Her lips clamped shut as her delicate features twisted with obvious confusion. "I'm sorry?"

"You asked why I call you 'princess'. It's not because I think you're spoiled." His throat worked a hard swallow. "It's because of your bed."

"My…bed."

Shadow's brows dipped toward the center as Slade ran a hand over his scruff-covered jaw. He was doing a piss poor job of making her understand, so he parted his lips and tried again.

"Before I left Charlotte to come find you in Ohio, your father gave me a file. In it was information about Stanton dating back to before his days working at that law firm with your mother. It also included a copy of the official police documents from her murder investigation."

"Okaaay..."

Explain better, dickhead.

"There were pictures in the file. Ones that showed the house you were living in at the time. One was of your bedroom. It was painted a light pink, and your bed was a twin-sized—"

"Princess bed." Shadow smiled fondly with a slow-moving nod. "I remember."

The blues in her eyes darkened, her stare softening with emotion he hadn't intended to conjure. But it was there, all the same, and Slade could feel himself becoming lost in her magnetic gaze.

The little girl she used to be was still in there. Still frozen in time, unable to break free from a trauma no child should ever have to endure.

Shadow's lips parted slightly, the movement pulling his attention away from her baby blues. The craving to taste her was instant and strong as she inched herself closer to where he stood frozen in place.

She didn't stop until her body was barely separated from his. And when she rose onto her sneakered tiptoes with a gentle lift of her delicate chin—

"Shadow..."

"Shh..." The defiant whisper was as entrancing as

the woman herself, making it impossible for him to pull away.

With a feathered touch, her lips brushed lightly over his, and though he knew he shouldn't, Slade couldn't help but accept what she had offered.

He reached up, sliding a palm against her flawless cheek. Shadow leaned into his touch, her lids falling shut as she brought herself closer to him.

More than ready to get lost in what he knew would be an incredible kiss, Slade placed a gentle hold on her hip and started to let his own eyes close. With his next breath, he pulled her body flush with his, and just as their lips pressed together for the very first time…

His phone began to ring.

They both froze, and it was all he could do not to yank the damn thing out of his pocket and throw it across the room. Instead, he dropped his hands back to his sides and removed himself from Shadow's personal space.

Instantly recognizing the ringtone, he let her know, "It's your father."

"Of course, it is," Shadow sighed, not bothering to hide her disappointment.

"I have to take it."

"I know." The smile she gave didn't come close to reaching her eyes. "It's okay. While you talk to him, I'm going to head upstairs and take a shower. When I come back down, I'll make us some food." She went for her bag, which was still on the dining room table, but as she started for the stairs, she stopped and turned back around. "There is food here, right?"

Despite his own feelings about the untimely interruption, Slade felt his lips twitch with the urge to smile. "Your father assured me the kitchen is fully stocked."

She held his stare a beat longer before giving a quick nod and turning away. Slade reached into his front pocket and pulled out his phone, watching from behind as she climbed the thick, log stairs.

"Garrison," he answered the call in his usual, gruff manner.

"I take it you two are getting settled in okay?"

Owens' ironically timed question had Slade studying the space around him as a moment of paranoia began to set in.

"We are," he answered the other man's question, quickly clearing his throat to avoid any semblance of nerves. "Shadow just headed upstairs for a quick shower, then we're going to have a bite to eat before calling it a night. I was about to do a perimeter sweep when you called."

Okay, so that last part was only partially true. He *had* been thinking about how he needed to check the security of the cabin's exterior, as well as the immediate area that surrounded it.

But then she'd looked up at him with those big, blue eyes and brought her mouth to his, and then…

And then, we almost kissed.

Technically, they *had* kissed, but only just barely because his damn phone had chosen that exact moment to start ringing. Now, Shadow was upstairs and stripping down naked while he was stuck down here, talking to her dad.

Probably a good thing, otherwise, who knows how far things would have gone?

A lot farther than a chaste, closed-lip kiss, that was for damn sure. And *that* was a complication he didn't fucking need.

"Good to hear it," Owens' deep voice filled the phone's speaker once more. "I wasn't sure how well my daughter would handle being locked away with you in the woods."

Despite his most recent thoughts, Slade found his muscles tensing defensively in response to the other man's comment. "Meaning?"

"At ease, Digger." His boss's British accent was more prominent than usual. "That wasn't intended as an insult, but rather a warning of sorts. Shadow's not the kind of woman who likes to be caged, as I'm sure you'll soon discover."

"Don't worry, sir," Slade assured the other man. "I'll make sure she's well-protected."

"Of that, I have no doubt. Truth be told, I'm just as worried about how *you'll* fare once this is all over and done with."

Me?

He frowned. "Why me?"

But rather than answer his question, Owens instead said, "Stay safe, Digger. I'll touch base with you again in the morning. If you need anything before then, you know how to reach me."

"Copy that."

A second later, the phone went silent, letting him know his boss had just ended the call.

Slade blew out a breath and shoved his phone back into his pocket as the sound of running water turned his attention to the top of the stairs. Doing his best to ignore the fact that she was up there right now, wet and naked, he headed that way to let her know he'd be outside.

His booted feet hit the bottom step, and he didn't slow his pace until he'd reached the top. He followed the sound of the water, turning right, and continuing to the room at the end of the hall.

Since the bedroom door had been left half-open, he called out her name and waited. When there wasn't an answer, Slade took a quick peek, just in case she hadn't gone into the shower just yet.

After a quick scan of the room, his gaze slid toward the bathroom door on his left. It, too, had been left slightly open, but only by a couple of inches. He padded across the carpeted floor and lifted a fist to knock.

"Yeah?" Shadow's voice reached him through the sound of rushing water.

"I'm going to—" Slade's voice cracked, which was something that never happened. So he cleared his throat with a frown and started again. "I just wanted to let you know I'm going to do a perimeter check before I lock up for the night. I'll be right back."

"Okay," she hollered back, not sounding concerned about his leaving her alone in the least.

Given that she'd gone on a solo hunt for a killer, spending a few minutes alone in a secured cabin likely had no place on Shadow's spectrum of fear.

It was that lack of fear that prompted him to add, "I hope it goes without saying, but you need to stay inside while I'm out there."

"Not a problem," Shadow didn't hesitate to respond. "This shower feels too good to go anywhere at the moment."

Bet it would feel a whole lot better if I were in there with you.

Slade nearly choked on the thought—and the erotic picture it brought forth. Turning his head, he started to leave when movement caught his attention from the corner of his eye.

On reflex, he looked back, inadvertently glancing through the narrow space between the door's edge. He stopped mesmerized by what he could see in the partially-fogged bathroom mirror.

Holy shit.

He knew he should look away, but his eyes refused

to let him. It was as if they were being held hostage by the image filling the reflective glass.

Mounted opposite of what appeared to be an impressively large shower, the mirror allowed him to see only a sliver of the woman standing inside. Her image was covered in a layer of steam that had clouded the shower's glass door.

Part of him felt ashamed for watching her like that without her knowledge or permission. But the other part of him…the primal, male part that was filled with a longing like none he'd ever known… couldn't help but cherish the stolen glance.

His heart kicked against his ribs as the sight of her beautifully blurred silhouette stole his breath the second she came into view. Committing the moment to memory, he could only just make out the gentle curves of her body.

Her shoulders and the dip of her waist. Hips he could see himself holding beneath the grip of his palms. Legs he longed to have wrapped around him while he drove himself harder and deeper into her hot, wet—

No.

Slade looked away, nearly releasing a growl of self-loathing for even having those thoughts. This was Shadow for Christ's sake. He shouldn't be stealing a peek at her in the shower…or anywhere else for that matter.

Probably shouldn't have kissed her downstairs, either then, huh?

Wanting to kick his own ass—for the sort-of kiss and a multitude of other reasons—he marched out of the room and back down the stairs. Step after forceful step, Slade didn't stop until he was fully outside, standing in the middle of the cabin's front porch.

He sucked in as big a breath as his lungs would physically allow. Images he shouldn't want to see filled his head, and he forced them away with a single, hard shake. Then he went back inside, reset the alarm, and shut the door behind him as he crossed the threshold once again.

Double-checking that the lock had automatically engaged, he pulled the pistol from its concealed holster at his right hip. With his attention back on keeping her safe, rather than getting her into his bed, Slade looked around at the scene before him.

He was met with nothing but the darkening sky, thick trees, and a small yard filled with well-trimmed grass. The evening air had grown colder even in the short time they'd been inside, but he used the chilling breeze to help sharpen his senses…and keep his mind far from distraction.

Slade went to the right, his gun held tightly in his fist as his head moved on a constant swivel. The dense woods that surrounded the structure was a double-edged sword, offering both the cover they needed to keep the cabin hidden away from prying eyes, but also the perfect hiding place for the enemy.

The chances of anyone finding them out here were less than slim to none, but that didn't keep him from ensuring the area was secure. There wasn't any room for error with any job he and the team took on.

Especially not with this one.

Because again, this was Shadow. The woman who watched over him and the other Tac-Ops men every time their boots hit the field. Her work may be done thousands of miles away from a computer, but that didn't make her any less vital of a member of their team.

Even if she wasn't a part of Tac-Ops, however—or his boss's daughter—Slade would still do whatever it took to keep the sexy blonde safe. Not simply because it was a job he'd been assigned or an order he'd agreed to follow, but because despite the fact that they'd only recently truly met, he couldn't imagine his life without her in it.

And there was a man out there who wanted Shadow dead. A man willing to risk everything he'd worked for his entire life in order to make that happen.

Anyone with as much power and political pull as Senator Stanton had to be desperate to attempt such a potentially damning move. And he knew as well as anyone, desperate men were some of the scariest of all.

They were unpredictable, making their decision and the consequences that followed, impossible to foresee. While those with nothing to lose could be every bit as dangerous, a guy like Stanton—a former CIA assassin with enough friends and money to back up his cause—made Slade more fearful than any of the terrorists he and his team had chased.

But as he continued checking the rest of the perimeter, Slade knew the fear he was currently feeling had nothing to do with self-preservation and everything to do with the thought of something happening to the woman waiting inside.

Speaking of Shadow…

He climbed the front steps and entered the code on the exterior keypad connected to the cabin's state-of-the-art security system. The tiny light at the top turned green as the locks audibly disengaged, and he opened the door and stepped over the threshold once more.

Shutting the door behind him, he went to the interior keypad and entered the same code. With the alarm active and ready to alert them of anyone stupid enough to try to break in, Slade turned and started for the stairs.

He made it three whole steps before he froze mid-stride, the sight of Shadow walking down the steps toward him momentarily stealing his ability to even think.

Fresh from the shower, her long hair lay damp

around her shoulders and the top portion of her arms. Her face was free of all signs of makeup, and she looked much more relaxed and comfortable in a pair of black leggings and an oversized t-shirt.

Slade wasn't sure how it was possible, but somehow she looked even more beautiful than before. But one thing he did know—the only thing that seemed to be perfectly clear—was that, when it came to this woman, he was in serious, serious trouble.

CHAPTER 6

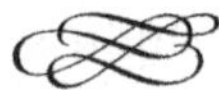

SHADOW'S HEART GAVE A HARD KICK WHEN SHE SAW Digger looking up at her from the cabin's front entrance. He was just standing there, staring back at her with an unreadable gaze, and all she could think was…

I want to kiss him again.

To be fair, they hadn't really kissed the first time. At least, not in the way she'd always imagined. Her father's killer timing was to blame for the untimely interruption.

Though she hated to admit it, the missed opportunity was probably for the best. It would be different if they were here on a romantic getaway for two. Unfortunately for her, that was far from being the case.

A killer was out there, walking around as a free and powerful man. And though she may be on temporary lockdown with her own personal bodyguard watching over her every move, she had no intentions of giving up on a fight that had only just begun.

As for what came after, well…that remained to be seen.

"Hey." She added a slight bounce to her steps and her best British accent to her tone. "I take it you didn't find the Boogeyman hiding in the bushes during your evening jaunt around the cabin."

Rather than smile, as had been her hope, Digger's handsome face dipped into an inexplicably frustrated scowl.

"No." He gave a curt shake of his head before resuming his previous steps in her direction. "The perimeter's clear."

Alrighty, then.

Assuming his extra grumpy mood had something to do with her having initiated their earlier, sort-of kiss, Shadow took his foul mood as a sign to move on as if it never happened.

"You still hungry?" She reached the bottom of the steps. "I thought I'd whip something up for us while you got cleaned up."

"I could eat." Digger stopped moving once again, keeping himself a safe distance away.

Okay, so apparently he's back to his usual stay-the-hell-away-from-me self. Good to know.

The idea of apologizing for her previously flirtatious behavior briefly entered Shadow's mind, but then she remembered this was Digger. If it wasn't one thing souring the man's stoic demeanor, it was another. And since he didn't appear to be keen on sharing whatever it was that had him scowling this time, Shadow ignored the elephant in the room and shot him her most casual, breeziest smile.

"Great!" She purposely sounded far cheerier than she felt. "You go shower, and I'll scrounge us up some food."

She didn't have to inquire about any possible allergies, as she'd had access to his and the other Tac-Ops members' medical records for years. There also wasn't a question as to the man's pickiness when it came to the food he consumed. Her involvement in the team's operations had long ago taught her Digger would either eat what was available or choose to go without.

A low grunt was all the response she was given as the two split off in separate directions. He went up the stairs with his bag slung over one of his broad shoulders while Shadow headed to the kitchen she'd caught a glimpse of earlier.

Positioned at the back of the cabin, the space was as pretty as the rest of the rustic hideaway. The large island and cabinets had been stained to match the floors.

The collection of stainless-steel appliances were nice enough to impress even a professional chef. Shadow smiled when she noticed a portion of the kitchen's far wall that showcased several cast-iron skillets hanging from matching black hooks.

Her father had always enjoyed being away from the city, hence his decision to purchase a plantation versus a high-rise apartment. She could remember the occasional camping trips they'd taken whenever she was a child…and he'd always cooked the fish they caught in a skillet like the ones she was staring at now.

But even then, the nightmare of what had happened to her mother was always present. And like then, those memories were still a permanent, horrifying fixture. Their flashes striking her at the most random of times.

Because every memory she shared with her father, no matter how wonderful, or sweet, or loving they may be, were reminders of what had always been missing…and of her mother's untimely death at the hands of a cold-blooded killer.

Shadow blinked against the stinging in her eyes as she looked away from the pans and started for the fridge. The past was the past, and there wasn't anything she could do to change it. She would, however, do whatever she could to destroy Stanton's future.

But for now…

She turned and headed for the oversized refrigerator. With her focus once again on making her and Digger some dinner, she opened the double doors and began perusing the contents, which had been placed inside. Her smile returned when she found it fully stocked, just as her father had promised.

For drinks, there were several bottles of water and chilled cans of her favorite diet soda. Various types of her favorite fresh fruits and veggies filled two of the three drawers while the one in the center held packages of lunch meats and cheeses.

But it was what she found on the middle shelf that piqued her interest most of all.

Shadow reached inside and grabbed the bundle wrapped neatly in brown butcher paper. Her smile grew even more when she read the familiar label.

Yes!

Knowing she didn't have much time, she went straight to work prepping the food. The first thing she did was to gather up the rest of the ingredients, and after that, she began to peel, slice, chop, and julienne.

With the cabbage prepped and the homemade pico mixed and marinating in the fridge, she made the sauce that put this recipe over the top. Shadow quickly unwrapped the butcher paper to reveal two pounds of freshly bought shrimp. She then peeled and deveined half of the generous portion before seasoning it the way she always did when making this particular dish.

The upstairs shower was turned off, letting her know her dinner guest would be joining her very soon. She hurried to place the seasoned shrimp inside the air fryer tucked away in one corner of the counter, setting the temp and the timer, thankful it would only take seven minutes for the shrimp to cook.

Lucky for her, Digger had taken a longer-than expected shower, and the extra time he'd spent in the bathroom worked greatly in her favor. Shadow moved quickly to finish getting everything ready as she set the table with plates and silverware for two. By the time he came down the stairs to join her, dinner was ready to be served.

"Perfect timing." Shadow smiled as she stood by the chair she'd chosen for herself, doing everything in her power to school her expression.

Because damn if the man didn't look even sexier than before.

His short, brown hair appeared slightly darker due to the strands still being wet. The skin covering his cheeks just above his short beard was flush from what she assumed was the shower's hot steam.

But oddly, it was the black hoodie and gray sweats that turned her on the most.

She wasn't sure what it was about a man in a hoodie, but damn if she didn't find it sexy as sin. Especially one who looked as good as Digger, who was still looking at her, rather than the meal waiting to be consumed.

The idea that a man in gray sweats made women all over the globe drop their panties was a familiar and, in her opinion, an oversold cliché. But a cliché's very existence is depended upon things happening so often they *become* cliches, so…

She watched Digger made his way toward her in those mouthwatering sweats.

Lord, have mercy.

"I made shrimp tacos," she blurted out the obvious before clearing her throat and trying again. "I hope that's okay."

He finally pulled his eyes away from hers to scan the spread she'd carefully arranged. "Looks good," Digger rumbled low as he pulled out the wooden chair across from where she still stood. "Thank you."

"You're welcome." Shadow took a seat before starting to fill her plate.

She put a generous amount of the slaw into three of the available soft taco shells.. This was followed by a drizzle of the savory—and slightly spicy—sauce, some pico, and four perfectly cooked shrimp.

Once Digger was finished filling his plate, Shadow took the very first bite. On reflex, her eyelids fell shut as she moaned, her tastebuds never tiring of what was one of her very favorite shrimp creations.

The man sitting across from her cleared his throat before taking a massive bite. When he was finished chewing, his throat worked to shove it all down before he grabbed the bottle of water she'd provided and taking a giant swig.

"I can't tell if you're trying to scarf your food

because you don't like it, and you're just trying to power through, or—"

"No, it's good." His next bite nearly finished the other half of the taco in his hands. "Really good, actually."

That last part was added while the food was still in his mouth, making Shadow inwardly giggle. On the outside, however, she decided to razz him just a tad. After all, it wasn't every day that she got the opportunity to do so face-to-face.

"You don't have to sound so surprised, you know." She feigned a scowl and pretended he'd hurt her feelings. "I do have other talents outside the realm of technology. I can cook, catch and clean fish, play the piano, change a tire, sew on a button—"

"You play the piano?" Digger seemed to marvel a bit at that particular revelation.

"Since I was five. I took lessons for several years, but once I got into high school, my obsession with using computers to uncover deeply hidden information overshadowed pretty much every other interest I had at the time. But I still tickle the ivories now and again."

She waggled her fingers in the air as if they were striking an invisible piano's keys.

"Impressive." The sexy man nodded, sounding genuine in his sentiment.

So naturally, Shadow had no choice but to take advantage of the rare moment.

"Oh, that's nothing." She leaned forward, lowering her voice to a deeper, sultrier tone. "When it comes to these babies"—she lifted her hands again with a playfully arched brow—"my talents are endless."

Digger choked on the sip of water he'd been attempting to swallow, barely managing to keep the liquid from spewing from his mouth. Though she wanted to burst out laughing at his reaction, Shadow offered him a napkin from the small stack she'd carried in from the kitchen instead.

"Was it something I said?"

Rather than answer, Digger grabbed the napkin and wiped the beard around his lips dry. "Do you ever take anything seriously?" he challenged with a frustrated frown.

She swallowed back the bubble of laughter working its way up her throat. "Of course, I do. I just don't take *everything* seriously. You know, studies have shown that smiling and laughing are very good for your health."

"Is that so?"

"It's true. Scientists have proven that smiling and laughing triggers the reward part of your brain which, in turn, releases endorphins. Everybody knows endorphins help with pain control. They serve as mood stabilizers and can do wonders for stress and anxiety." Then, because she couldn't help herself, Shadow added a quipped, "You should give it a try sometime."

"I laugh," he argued, even as the dip of his dark brows grew deeper.

The unladylike snort that came from her body practically echoed off the cabin's thick walls. "Sorry to be the one to break it to you, big guy, but a grunt does not a laugh make."

Digger opened his mouth to no doubt pop back with some sort of grumbly, grimaced retort. But at the last minute, he closed those lips she hadn't had enough time to really taste and went for another taco, instead.

After what felt like a very long, very uncomfortable silence, the former SEAL continued the conversation by opening up to her in a way she'd never expected.

"I don't know how you do it." His deep rumble was quieter than usual.

When he didn't elaborate, Shadow wasted no time prompting him for more.

"How I do what?" She abandoned the partially eaten taco in her hand, setting its remnants down onto her plate.

"Ignore it all."

"Umm…you're going to have to give me a little more than that."

His brown eyes lifted from his empty plate to her. The intensity in his gaze as it became locked with hers caused a tightness within her chest.

"All you've been through…what happened with

your mother, and then having your entire life uprooted to move to Charlotte by a dad who lied to you about what he and your mother both did for a living…"

"I've known about my father's past work as a government spy since I was a teenager."

"But you only just found out about your mother being in the CIA a few hours ago."

"What's your point?"

He leaned forward, resting both elbows on the table. "My point is, you get hit with some pretty big news, and yet you're sitting here cracking jokes as if this were any other day."

"It is any other day, Digger." Her expression became serious. "Think about the work we do. The things you and your team have been forced to see and endure. If you let all that bad mojo screw with your head, you'd be about as useful in the field as a toddler with a squirt gun."

"So what, you're saying all the jokes and smartass responses are your way of coping?"

"Absolutely." Shadow was already nodding before he'd finished the question. "Listen, I learned a long time ago that sitting in the corner and crying does nothing but bring me more sorrow and pain. And it sure as hell won't bring my mother back or take down the man who killed her. So I choose to smile and to laugh every chance I get. I *choose* to find humor in situations that most people probably wouldn't. Because if

I don't…if I let my mother's death become all-consuming, then there won't be enough of me left to go after the man responsible. And I have to bring him down, Dig. He can't keep getting away with what he did."

Several seconds passed as they sat there, staring into one another's eyes without uttering a single word. And this time, when Digger spoke up once again, it wasn't to ask about her or her horrifying past, but instead he began to tell her more about him.

"You've probably already looked into the team's backgrounds." He settled back against his chair. "Hell, you probably know more about me than I do at this point."

"Maybe," she answered truthfully. "But old police reports and military records only give a girl so much. I'd really like it if you were the one who filled in all the blanks."

He paused, that entrancing gaze of his studying hers a few seconds longer. And then those delectable lips parted, and he began to talk, sharing with her everything that had turned him into the man he was today.

"Well, let's see…I never knew who my real dad was. Still don't, actually. And I was four the first time I remember seeing my mom strung out on cocaine."

The tightening in her chest got worse. "That had to be a hard thing to see. Especially as a little boy."

"I remember being worried that she was having

some sort of medical issue because she was in such a manic state. At the time, I didn't know that word even existed. I just knew that something wasn't quite right. When I'd ask, all she'd say was that she'd taken her 'feel good' medicine her doctor had prescribed."

"And I'm sure, as a kid, you took her at her word."

Digger nodded. "Doctors do good, right? They're supposed to help make people better. So yeah, I figured if that's where the so-called medicine came from, then it must be okay."

"When did you figure out that it wasn't?"

"About a year later."

"When you were five."

Another nod. "I came home from kindergarten one day and found her strung out on the living room floor. The needle was still sticking out of her arm, and I thought…" His Adam's apple bobbed with a hard swallow. "I was sure she was dead."

"I'm so sorry."

"Oh, it gets better." His broad shoulders shook with a humorless laugh. "Of course, you already know what happened with the whole—"

"Tell me anyway," she encouraged softly.

With another working of his throat, Digger pulled in a deep breath and gave her the shortened version of his heartbreaking childhood.

"I started getting bounced around the foster care system so she could try her hand at rehab. She'd do better for a while. Those first few weeks back, she was like Mother of the Fucking Year. But then she'd fallen back into old habits, and once that happened..."

"The cycle would start all over again."

His nod was slight, his expression one of acceptance. But there was also love for a mother lost to him too soon, as well as some residual resentment and anger still brewing behind his dark, stoic gaze.

"Tell me about the men," she prodded softly after the next stretch of silence became too deafening to bear.

"What about them?" He scowled. "They were a bunch of losers who were just as bad-off as she was, only their list of addictions included paying my mother for sex."

"That's how she ended up in jail, right? Weren't you six when she was arrested and charged with prostitution?"

A sarcastic smile lifted one corner of his lips. "At the time, I remember thinking it would have been better if she'd actually died, rather than having a mom who was in prison. But then...something happened. After two years of being behind bars, my mom was finally, truly clean."

Just as he'd accused, Shadow already knew the rest of the heartbreaking story. But she hadn't lied when she'd said she wanted to hear it from his perspective, and when he finally opened up, she couldn't help but share in his pain.

"Believe it or not, we had some good times after

that." His mouth curved into a ghost of a smile even as a flash of sadness filled his gaze. "She was released when I was eight, and for the first six months, I stayed with a foster family while she came for scheduled, supervised visits. Her parole officer helped her find a steady job, and with assistance from a community outreach program for parolees, she was approved for a two-bedroom apartment."

"Is that when you started living with her again?"

"Yeah." He took a sip of his water before continuing. "The place wasn't the best, but it was far better than the run-down shack we'd once lived in. And the best part was, for the first time in my life, I actually had a mom."

"I'm really sorry you lost her so soon after."

"Almost two years to the day after I moved back in with her." His gaze returned to hers. "I was at school when the counselor came and pulled me from my classroom. I was only ten, and our past was such a clusterfuck of chaos I was sure when I saw the police officers waiting for us in the principal's office that she'd fallen back off the wagon."

"But she hadn't." Shadow's vision blurred behind a well of unshed tears.

Her kindred heart broke for the boy who'd lost his mother at such a young age. Especially after all they'd been through to find their way back to one another.

"No." Digger's voice grew thick as his childhood story drew to a tragic end. "Some teenager coked out of his mind robbed the convenience store where she was working. The officers told me my mother did everything exactly right. She gave him the money from the cash register without arguing. She never tried to fight him off or threaten him in any way. And the kid…he just shot her at point-blank range as if she were nothing. When the cops asked him later why he'd done it, he said he'd killed her just because—"

"He could," she finished softly. Because yeah, she'd read the police report on his mother's death. But no matter how many times her eyes crossed over the printed words, they'd never made her feel the empathy or pain in her chest at his loss as she did in that very moment. "I'm so sorry, Slade." His nickname didn't seem fitting, given the story he'd just shared. "I know our stories aren't exactly the same, but I do understand how you feel. To a certain extent, at least."

She'd been lucky enough to have a loving and nurturing mother from even before she was born. But he'd only been given that for two very short years before a bullet ripped his mother away."

"I'm sorry."

His muttered apology took her by surprise.

"For what?"

"Making the conversation all about me."

"You didn't." Shadow shook her head. "I *asked* you to talk about your past. And I know it isn't an easy thing to dredge up. Trust me, there are days I wish my past was all some sort of terrifying dream, but..." Her words trailed off with a shake of her head before she looked deep into his eyes and said, "It really means a lot that you were willing to share all of that with me."

"Not sure why I did, to be honest."

For some reason, this made her smile. "Perhaps because you aren't strong enough to resist my charming ways."

"Or maybe you put some sort of truth serum in the pico without my knowledge or consent."

Shadow blinked, and it took her a full two seconds to realize...

"Did you just make a joke?"

His deadpan expression told her everything she needed to know.

"Holy shit, you did. You, the infamous smiling-is-for-pussies Digger just made an actual joke. I mean, on a scale of one to hilariously funny, it maybe rates at like...a six. But still, you put yourself right out there, and I for one am so proud to know that—"

"Shadow?"

"Yes?"

"Shut up and finish your food."

The man's words may have been gruff and a tad bit rude, but the small smirk she saw sent her lips curving into a full-blown grin. For the remainder of their time at the table, they took turns sharing more about themselves and their lives prior to working for Tac-Ops.

Digger volunteered even more about himself, and the years following his mother's death. He gave his thoughts about growing up in the system, his struggles at school, and how glad he was that he'd joined the Navy right after graduation.

Shadow shared more about what her life was like prior to her mother's murder. Memories of her mom, and some funny ones involving her dad.

Long after the food had vanished from their plates, the two were still sitting at the table swapping stories as if they were each trying to one-up the other in a competition of the funniest story.

A rush of warmth quickly spread throughout her entire system as she listened to him tell of antics pulled by him and the rest of the team. The longer they talked, the more they shared. And when one particularly hysterical story involving her teenage self nearly getting caught hacking into her high school's online grading system, the most wonderful, magical, surprising thing happened…

Slade "Digger" Garrison threw his head back and laughed.

All sense of time and space around her slowly began to dissolve. For the second time in her life—the first being when her mother was shot and killed—Shadow felt as though her entire world had just tilted on its axis.

Beautiful.

It wasn't nearly an adequate enough word to describe the sight before her, but she couldn't seem to think of another that fit the bill. Digger's chin was up, his eyes squeezed tight, and the opened mouth smile he wore spread clear across his handsome face.

But it was his laugh—that deep, manly, reverberating laugh—that consumed the air around them. It was hands-down the most beautiful sound ever to have reached her ears. And as Shadow sat there, soaking up every last second of the incredible, stolen moment, she felt as though she'd been given a gift that had just changed her heart forever.

Oh, this could be bad. Really, really bad.

Or it could end up even better than she'd ever dreamed.

* * *

"I FOUND HER."

Michael Stanton sat up a little straighter as Doug Easton's voice sounded from the burner phone's speaker. Giving his locked office door a second glance, he kept his voice low so anyone who happened to enter the hallway outside couldn't possibly overhear.

"Where?"

"Charlotte."

Ah, so she ran back home to Daddy.

He sat back in the expensive leather chair his

constituents paid for with their hard-earned taxes and smiled. "How sure are you?"

"One hundred percent," Doug's unwavering tone oozed of confidence. "I've had a guy watching the Travel Assurance building since the night of the shooting."

"I hope to hell this isn't the same idiot who let her get away the first time."

"No, that guy has already been taken care of."

Michael didn't ask for details because he didn't want to know. The only thing he needed to be certain of was that the loose end had been tied.

Speaking of loose ends…

"This man you have in Charlotte," he continued. "How do I know he can be trusted."

"You don't. But I do, and that's all that matters."

"Bullshit. You trusted the last asshole and look how that turned out."

"This guy's different."

"How so?"

Doug momentarily paused before adding, "Because he is with the Agency, too."

Not he was or used to be, but…

He is.

"Currently active?" Michael needed to be sure.

"Affirmative. And, he's good. Better than good, actually. If you'd like, I can send you a copy of his file."

"No." He shook his head despite the fact that

Doug couldn't see him. "The fewer trails there are to follow, the better."

"I agree." The other man cleared his throat. "Anyway, as I was saying, my guy was outside Rafe Owens' building earlier today when he spotted Alice Owens entering the building with one of her father's employees."

His cold heart thumped hard at the news. So it *was* the Owens girl he'd seen lurking outside three of his rallies and a fundraiser event, all held in Columbus over the course of the last two weeks.

At first, Michael had been flattered, believing he had a sexy, young new fan. But then he'd made the mistake of asking a member of his security team to sneak a few pictures without being noticed.

When he'd passed those along to Doug to run through the man's high-tech facial recognition system, he'd nearly fallen on his ass with shock.

Ninety-eight point six percent match to a girl who was supposed to be dead.

Michael had denied his friend's findings, ordering him to run her image through his system again. After three separate tries yielded the exact same results, he finally accepted the science for the truth that it was.

I spared the little bitch's life that night and for what? So she could come after me twenty-six years later?

Well, she wasn't a kid anymore. And whether the woman wanted money or revenge, it didn't matter. She wouldn't get the chance for either.

"You run him?" he asked of the man seen with the Owens woman.

"Facial rec got a hit," Doug confirmed. "Name's Slade Garrison, and he's a former Navy SEAL-turned-insurance salesman."

Insurance, my ass.

"What else do you know?"

"Guy's background is pretty thin. He entered the Navy right out of high school, then boot camp to BUD/S. According to what I've found out so far, Garrison was part of the most decorated SEAL unit on record. He was given an Honorable Discharge a few years ago, after which, he went to work for Owens."

As the other man's words sank in, everything suddenly began to make perfect sense.

"Owens knows about the shooting," Michael spoke his theory aloud.

"How can you be so sure?"

"The man is nothing if not a loving and protective father. If he thinks his daughter is in danger, he'll do whatever it takes to protect her."

"Including assigning his former SEAL employee as her personal protective detail," Doug surmised.

"Exactly. And if that's the kind of man watching over her, we'll need to approach this thing with caution."

"Don't worry." The other man did his best to reassure him. "I already have a plan in the works."

"You'd better."

"I tagged his car after they went inside the building," Doug let him know. "From what I can tell, both the woman are holed up in a cabin in the middle of the fucking woods."

"A cabin?" Michael frowned.

"Before you ask, I already checked out the property's deed. It's owned by a shell company with no known ties to Owens or any of his people, but given the guy's background…"

The other man didn't finish, but Michael already knew what Doug was thinking. A former MI6 operative would have no problem hiding the fact that he owned the wooded hideout.

"It's a safe house," he told his trusted confidant. It was the only thing that made sense. "At the very least, there will be an alarm system and cameras. And if this guy really was a SEAL—"

"Don't worry," Doug interrupted with an attempt at appeasement. "I'm putting a plan in place as we speak that will almost certainly draw them back into the city."

"Make it quick. And this time, make damn sure that it's done."

Rather than wait for the other man to give him an unnecessary response, Michael ended the call and shoved the phone back into the hidden bottom in one of his desk drawers. Locking it tight, he pushed himself up out of his chair and headed for his private bathroom.

He checked his watch on the way there to see how much time he had left before his next meeting. This one was with a group of Girl Scouts and their leader to discuss the importance of some sort of bullshit cause.

Michael smiled when he saw he had just enough time to grab a coffee on his way there.

CHAPTER 7

I'm dreaming.

Even in his subconscious state, Slade was aware that none of what was happening was real. Which was why he let the best fucking dream of his life continue because he was with her. He was with…

Shadow.

They were together in his bed, and the two of them were naked. Fueled by unbridled passion and hunger, their bodies became tangled in the sheets as he took her the way he'd always imagined.

Over and over, he drove himself deep into her core. She was hot and wet and staring up at him with those incredible eyes, and all he could think was that he was finally home.

But then something changed, and her expression turned from wild abandon to one filled with fear. And when she opened her mouth, it wasn't his name she cried out. Instead, he heard her shouting for—

"Help!"

Slade's eyes flew open, and he threw off the covers, shooting straight up in his bed. His chest heaved with heavy pants, just as it had been doing in his dream, and his dick was so full and hard the damn thing physically ached.

What the hell was that?

He ran a hand through his already-mussed hair while his sleep-ridden mind worked to figure out what exactly had woken him. When the answer came seconds later, it sent his heart racing and his hand reaching for his gun.

"Please…help!"

Shadow!

Her echoing scream had him leaping from his bed, gun in hand as he raced from his bedroom into the hall. With his weapon held tightly in his grip, he kept it up and at the ready. His bare feet covered the wooden floor separating his room from hers in the span of a few terrifying seconds.

Slade didn't go slow or even consider using stealth as he burst through the door and into the room. His pulse raced, and his trigger finger slid into place, ready to take out anyone daring to come after the woman he was protecting.

But a quick and efficient sweep of the shadowed

room—as well as the connected bathroom—he realized there was no intruder. There was only…

Shadow.

She was lying in the middle of the bed, her body thrashing about beneath the thick bedding. He lowered the gun and drew in a deep breath, letting it out slowly as he willed his heartbeat back into a normal rhythm.

With the knowledge that no one had broken in with the intent to do harm came clarity. And as Slade made his way toward the bed, he finally understood what was really going on.

She's having a nightmare.

His heart ached at the sight of Shadow's tortured expression and the distressing sounds she was making. Unlike before, he couldn't quite make out her pleading mumbles, but their message was crystal clear.

She was stuck in a terrifying dream of her own mind's making. One that he suspected was more a memory from her past, rather than a fictional dream.

He went to the bed, unwilling to let the heartbreaking scene continue on his watch. With his free hand, he carefully reached out, placing his palm on her blanket-covered thigh.

"Shadow," Slade whispered as her leg shifted beneath his gentle touch.

Her eyes remained closed as she shook her head against her pillow with a whimpering, "No."

Several strands of her long, blonde hair became strewn across her grimacing face. Not seeing any signs that she was close to waking up, he used a little more force and nudged her again.

"Shadow," he said her name more curtly in the hopes that she'd hear him.

When the struggle against a monster only she could see continued, Slade put his pistol on her nightstand and ended her suffering once and for all.

"Dammit, Shadow!" He yelled that time. "Wake the hell up!"

With his hands on her shoulders, he gave her a stern shake.

Her eyes flew open, but it wasn't his face that she was seeing. Slade knew this because, rather than shake off the remnants of what had been an obviously awful dream, she immediately began to fight.

Son of a…

Slade lifted his arms in front of his face to defend it from her flailing hands. The sound of her palms slapping against his skin echoed, and she got in a few good hits before he literally got the upper hand.

"Stop!" His voice boomed as he wrapped his fingers around both of her wrists. At the same time, he crawled up onto the bed and straddled her much like he did the very first time they met.

The sleep-driven fog in her widened gaze finally began to clear. It was quickly replaced by a blinking look of confusion as she lay still beneath his gentle yet firm hold.

"Digger?"

A sense of déjà vu struck hard as he stared down at her beautiful, frowning face. "You were having a bad dream."

While I was busy having one of the best of my existence.

His dick—which was still half-hard from his own imagined scenario—twitched behind his boxer briefs. Thanks to the moon-lit slit shining down on her through the bedroom's curtains, the tiny flash of awareness in her eyes was plain to see.

"I'm sorry I woke you," Shadow offered softly, her voice rougher than normal from sleep.

But he shook his head, keeping his eyes locked onto hers. "Nothing to apologize for, princess."

She smiled even as a single tear fell from the corner of one eye. "I haven't had one that bad for almost a week." Her voice cracked and her chin quivered. "I thought maybe they'd stopped, but apparently not."

It was obvious the amazing woman was doing everything in her power to not completely break down. Her show of strength made him like her even more than he already did, but it also pissed him the hell off.

"It's okay to cry, you know?" He purposely kept his tone gentle. "You don't always have to put on a brave face or do the whole tough-girl routine. Not with me."

Never with me.

Her watery gaze searched deep within his, and a moment later…she began to crumble.

Shadow's hiccupping sobs ripped his heart in two in a way nothing else ever had before. Without giving it a second thought, he slid his body from her trembling form. Then he pulled her back against his front in a comforting embrace.

"I'm s-sorry," she offered between hiccupping breaths. "I don't really know w-what that w-was."

"That was you letting go," Slade spoke softly near her ear. "Something tells me it's been a while."

Her lungs hitched with their effort to restore her breathing to a more normal pace, and for a moment he didn't think she was going to respond. But then, as the movement of her rising shoulders evened out, he heard her sweet voice once more.

"I haven't cried like that since I was a child."

"Then I'd say you were long overdue."

"Says a man who's probably never cried an adult day in his life."

Strawberries and cream filled his nostrils as he relished in the scent of her hair. Drawing in a deep breath, he released it slowly before giving her a tiny piece of his soul.

"I cried the day my mom overdosed, and again when she went to prison. There were a few times in a couple of the worst foster homes I was to, but I always waited until I was in the shower so no one would ever know."

"Slade…"

"It was years after that before I ever cried again," he told her truthfully. "The first time I lost a fellow serviceman during an overseas op."

A stretch of silence passed for so long, he started to think maybe she'd fallen asleep. But then she moved, turning her body around so that she faced him, her eyes red and slightly puffy as they lifted slowly to meet his.

"I'm sorry," she whispered an apology, not because of her crying jag, but rather the loss that he had suffered.

"It was a long time ago." He did his best to brush the painful memory away.

"Time doesn't heal all wounds, like people claim, Slade."

Ah, sweetheart.

Reaching up, he gently tucked a few wayward strands of hair behind her ear. Slade let his hand linger there a bit longer as the pad of his thumb feathered back and forth against her cheek.

"Maybe it's not supposed to," he mused. "Maybe those memories are still there because we're never supposed to forget."

"Just learn to live with them?" she questioned. "Is that what you're saying?"

He shrugged, keeping his hand in place and his eyes locked tightly with hers. "Every part of our past has shaped who we are today. Good and bad, alike. And…" Slade swallowed hard, uncertain about saying this very next part. But before he could talk himself out of it, he finished with, "I like you just the way you are."

A soft rush of air escaped her gaping lips. Shadow blinked several times, the moisture there glistening in the light of the moon.

"I like you, too," she whispered with a ghost of a smile. "Even when you get all growly like a bear."

"I don't growl," he argued, his brows dipping in the center with a frown.

The soft snort that followed did wonders to ease the tension in his neck.

"Um…okay, sure." Her tone was filled with sarcasm as she patted a palm against his bare chest. "We can go with that, if it makes you feel better."

"I *don't*." He held on to the claim as if it were law. But his insistence only added fuel to the fire.

Shadow laughed, her entire body shaking within his loose hold, but rather than piss him off, as even he would have expected, Slade found himself chuckling, too.

"Yeah, well, I wouldn't growl so much if you weren't such a stubborn, frustrating—"

"Watch it, buster." She gave his chest a playful slap.

But as she did, he grabbed her wrist in a gentle hold and lifted her arm in the air. "Pretty sure you're the one who needs to watch it," he warned.

A second later, his hand was beneath her arm, and then…he started to tickle.

"Slade, stop!" she screeched loudly, her voice becoming high pitched and filled with boisterous laughter.

Her body twisted and turned as she worked to free herself from his grasp, her luscious mouth opened wide as she giggled and pleaded for his mercy.

"Admit that I'm right, and I'll quit," he teased, not fully aware of just how wide his own smile had spread.

"Okay!" Shadow relented as he continued with the playful torture. "You're right, okay? I'm stubborn, and frustrating, and sarcastic, and—"

His mouth slammed against hers to keep her from saying another word, his hands moving from torment to something much better. Because she may be all those things and more, but this woman was also absolutely…

Perfect.

Slade felt her entire body freeze beneath his touch half a second before Shadow melted into his arms. Her tongue met his in an explosion of pleasure, their lips matching in a dance that he never wanted to end.

He grunted, and she moaned, the sound wistful and matching the same need as his own. Her nails dug into the skin at his back, and his hips reflexively pressed against hers.

His lips moved from her mouth to her jaw, and below in a trail of hungry kisses. Shadow arched her back below him as if her body was begging him for more, so he slid a hand beneath the white tank-top she'd changed into before crawling into bed.

The soft, plump flesh of her breast fit perfectly against his palm. Shadow gasped when his fingertips found the taut nipple he toyed with while giving the side of her neck a gentle nibble.

"Slade…" She panted his name like a prayer.

He'd grant every single wish she had if he could.

But since he wasn't a genie, he did the next best thing and shoved her shirt up to expose both of her perfectly proportioned breasts. He took but a second to appreciate her natural beauty before leaning down and taking one of the hardened peaks between his lips.

Shadow cried out, her body bucking beneath his before spreading her legs wider to accommodate his muscular thighs. Slade took his fill, first one plump globe and then the other. And while he was giving the other breast the same ravenous attention, he slid his hand lower until his fingertips dipped beneath the elastic waist of her cotton panties.

Her pelvis lifted from the mattress in search of the pleasure he was more than willing to give. Slade filled his hand with her sex, loving that it was silky smooth and bare. His fingers began to explore, tracing her feminine curves and dips. He moved lower to the entrance of her hot, wet core, and then—

The sound of a light banging from outside reached his ears. Half a beat later, the cabin's high-end security system's alarm blared to life.

Son of a…

In one swift move, he removed the one hand from her panties and the other from her breast. Pushing himself up and over, he hopped down from the bed on his way to grab his gun.

"Where are you going?" Shadow threw off the covers and stood beside her bed.

He picked up his pistol from the nightstand, not bothering to check for a full mag or one in the chamber. That had already been previously confirmed.

"That was out back," he answered on his way to her door. Without looking back, he ordered a gruff, "Stay here. Lock the door, and don't open it for anyone but me."

"Slade, wait—" she called after him as he exited the room.

But he ignored her and shut the door, hoping like hell she did as she was told.

His mind raced as he ran down the stairs wearing nothing but his boxers and carrying his gun. It was implausible to think that anyone outside the team knew they were there. But this was Shadow, so he wasn't about to risk her safety by making a dumbass assumption.

He quickly disarmed the security system, the ear-piercing alarm cutting off as he opened the cabin's front door. It was the middle of the night, but the exterior lights were all motion activated, so when he stepped out onto the porch, everything within his immediate area was within view.

Thankful for its automatic lock system, Slade shut the door and moved as he'd trained, his eyes sweeping back and forth with efficiency and ease. Seeing nothing but the shadows of slightly blowing trees, he followed the same path he had before and went to his right.

The noise he'd heard while he and Shadow were in the midst of a hot and heavy make-out session had sounded as if it had come from around back. The grass was cold beneath his bare feet, his steps purposeful and silent as he followed the structure's southernmost wall.

Slade stopped and waited before rounding the corner. Gun in hand, he took in a deep breath, steadying his weapon and preparing himself for whatever he may find.

With his weapon held tightly out in front of his near-naked body, he rounded the corner just as he had countless times with his team in the field. The lights mounted near each corner of the roof's guttered edge illuminated the back patio and beyond.

It took mere seconds for him to assess the situation, and he soon realized there was no actual threat. Not to Shadow, at least. But the two metal trash cans that had been positioned up against the wall, well…

Those were a different story.

"You've got to be kidding me."

Slade watched as two round-bellied raccoons scurried away from the overturned cans. They were empty, but their scent had apparently piqued the animals' interest enough for them to have wanted to investigate further.

He stormed across the grouted pavers and righted the cans with his left hand while still holding his gun at his side. With their lids re-secured, he continued checking the rest of the area, because again, the woman inside wasn't one he was willing to risk.

Minutes later, Slade was back inside and the security system was once again reactivated. Heading straight upstairs, he didn't stop until he got to Shadow's bedroom. And when he tried opening the door, he was pleased to find it locked.

"It's me," he announced after tapping his knuckles against the smooth wood.

The sound of soft footfalls reached him seconds before she unlocked it, and her gorgeous face appeared.

"You just let two masked intruders walk away?" She stared up at him with a teasing smirk and a light click of her tongue. “My father is not going to be happy.”

“Very funny.” He made no move to re-enter the room. “I take it you were watching out the window?”

“Computer, actually.” Shadow slid to the side, revealing an open laptop resting in the middle of the bed. “I hacked into the cabin’s security feed the second you left. I could see the adorable creatures before you even made it outside.”

“You didn’t think to tell me?”

“And miss all the fun?”

Digger scowled, but he was more upset with himself than with her. *He* should’ve thought to check the feed before storming off half-naked into the dead of night.

You didn’t think about it because you were too busy focusing on other things. Namely the woman standing less than a foot away in nothing but a thin tank-top and barely-there panties.

His inner voice was right. He hadn’t thought things through as clearly as he should have because he’d done something he never did on a job…

I got distracted.

Not once in all his years as a SEAL, nor during his time with Tac-Ops had Slade ever let himself become distracted by a pretty face. And he’d damn sure never gotten physical with a woman he was charged with protecting.

But he had with Shadow. The last woman in the world he ever wanted to see get hurt.

Slade had given in to the need he felt for her without any regard for her safety or the very real threat that existed. If it had been an intruder and not just a pair of fucking raccoons, the night could have ended badly…for everyone involved.

She could have been hurt or even killed because he'd been too busy taking what he wanted instead of being the protector she deserved. Well, that shit stopped now. From this point on, his focus would be on keeping her safe and nothing more.

This was Shadow. She was his boss's daughter and part of his team. And despite the inexplicable spell the woman had somehow cast upon him, he was strong enough to ignore it. He *had* to be.

Her life depended on it.

"Are you going to stand there all night, or…"

"I think it's best if I go back to my own room," he answered gruffly.

The look of disappointment on her face was nearly enough to change his mind.

"Oh. Okay." She quickly flashed him a casual smile. "Whatever floats your boat, big guy. I'll just be here…lying in that big bed all alone…"

Her tone was as tempting as the woman herself, but Slade shoved his desires down and forced himself to stand his ground.

"I'm sorry, Shadow. What happened earlier was—"

"Just a taste of what could happen if you stay the night in here, instead."

He wanted nothing more than to do just that. But rather than give in to the urge to pick up right where they'd left off, Slade made his intentions from that moment forward crystal clear.

"This can't happen." He shook his head. "I'm supposed to be protecting you, not…"

"Shoving your tongue down my throat?"

Jesus. "I'm serious, Shadow. You're in danger, and I can't allow myself to be distracted."

"Is that what I am?" She inched closer. "A distraction?"

"I think you know you're more than that. But it doesn't matter. Me and relationships…they don't work. I'm just not built like the other guys. So I think it's best if we end whatever this is now, before shit goes sideways and someone winds up getting hurt."

Her baby blues blinked as her gaze widened with a nod. "Okay, well, first of all, I'm glad you think of me as more than just a distraction. And second…who said anything about a relationship? Because in case you didn't notice, I'm not exactly a long-term kinda gal, myself. So if you're worried that I'm going to get all clingy and needy just because we spend one night together—"

"It's not that." Slade shook his head.

"No? Then what is it? Because I know it's not that

you don't want me." Her gaze lowered to the bulge still throbbing between his thighs.

"You're right." There was no point in trying to lie. "I do want you. More than I've ever wanted another woman in my life."

"But?"

"But I respect the hell out of you and what you do for our team."

When he didn't say more, her brows dipped in the center with obvious confusion. "You see, your words sound like a really nice, really sweet compliment. But your tone makes me think you're using your respect for me as an excuse not to stay."

"Because I am," he admitted. He started to lift a hand, to reach for her as a lover would. But he stopped himself at the last second, pulling back to keep from falling back under her spell. "I can't…" Slade swallowed hard, clearing his throat before moving on. "I won't let my personal feelings toward you interfere with my ability to do my job. And if I stay—"

"Please stay."

He ground his back teeth together to keep from shouting out a resounding *yes*. "I'm not the man for you, Shadow. Casual or otherwise." A slow shake of his head. "I'm sorry."

Turning his back on the one thing he wanted more than anything else in the world, Slade started to leave for the bedroom down the hall but was stopped mid-stride by the sound of her sweet voice.

"Don't you think that's for me to decide?" she asked from her doorway.

"I'm sorry," he rumbled once more without turning around. But then, as if he couldn't keep from it, Slade looked back at her from over his shoulder and confessed, "I can't look at you and not want. And I'm not a fucking saint. I touch you like that again, there will be no stopping. Which will only make it harder on us both when this is over, and we have to walk away."

Their gazes remained locked on one another's for several long, agonizing seconds. But then Shadow's expression slowly changed from a look of desire to acceptance, and with a slight dip of her chin, she stopped begging him to stay.

"Goodnight, Digger." She went back to using his nickname. "And....just so you know...no matter what does or doesn't happen between us, I'm...really glad you're here."

Slade watched as she moved backward just enough to shut herself in for the night. And when the door snicked closed, and he could no longer see her, he couldn't help but wonder if he'd just made the biggest mistake of his life.

CHAPTER 8

Two days later…

"We come bearing gifts."

Slade kept his hand on the door he'd just opened as Bones and Falcon stared back at him from where they stood on the porch.

"What's that?" He eyed the two bulging bags Bones was holding at his sides.

But rather than waiting for an invitation, the other man took it upon himself to squeeze his way past.

"Lunch," his teammate answered only after he was fully inside.

While he put the bags onto the rustic dining room table, Falcon shot Slade a look and an unapologetic shrug. Slade sighed, moving further to the side to make room for the former Army Ranger to enter.

"We have food here," he grumbled as he shut the door and reset the alarm.

Bones reached into one of the bags and pulled out something wrapped in deli paper he recognized on sight. "Yes, but do you have *these?*"

"You brought us Petruccelli's?"

His initial annoyance at their unannounced visit all but vanished with the ill-timed growling of his stomach. A small, family-owned deli not far from where they worked, Petruccelli's was one of Charlotte's best-kept secrets.

"I got you the Porchetta, of course." Bones handed him the wrapped sandwich still in his hand. "I wasn't sure what Shadow would want..." He reached back into the sacks and began pulling out the remainder of the food. "So I picked up a meatball sub, focaccia caprese, and an Italian hoagie sub."

"Speaking of, where is Shadow, anyway?" Falcon's gaze scanned the parts of the cabin within their view.

"Upstairs." Slade set his sandwich down onto the table before turning and heading that way. "I'll go get her."

But before he could even make it to the first step, a bellowing Bones yelled her name to get her attention, instead.

"Hey, Shadow!" The other man cupped both sides of his mouth as he shouted for her again. "Come on down and get yourself some grub!"

"Jesus, Bones." Slade faced his teammate with a deep scowl. "I said I was going to go get her."

"I know." Bones shrugged. "But why waste all those extra steps when hollering for her works just as well?" Right on cue, his gaze slid to the top of the stairs. And when he lifted a hand and pointed in that direction, the medic flashed him an I-told-you-so grin. "See?"

He looked toward the top of the stairs at the same time Shadow appeared. She looked first to him, but as she'd done the last two days, her beautiful gaze quickly skittered away.

"Hey, guys." She turned her attention to Bones and Falcon as she started down the stairs. Her focus shifted to the food set out on the table. "What's all this?

"Petruccelli's," Bones responded proudly. "We figured after being stuck out here for the past few days, you'd be ready for a change."

Appreciation lit up her gorgeous face. "Are you kidding? I *love* that place!" Her steps quickened to cover the distance between her and the food at a faster pace.

"The sandwiches are marked," Falcon informed her. "Dig's is the Porchetta, but the others are up for grabs. Bones and I aren't picky, so whichever two you don't want, we'll take. Oh, and there are bottles of water in the bag on the left."

"Thank you so much." She grabbed the Caprese

and a bag of chips before plopping down into one of the table's six chairs.

The scent of strawberries lingered in her path, and Slade hated how much he was coming to love the fruity, sweet scent.

Bones picked up one of the remaining sandwiches before sitting in the chair closest to where he stood. "Our pleasure." He began to unwrap his selection.

"We also figured y'all might be getting a little stir-crazy." Falcon chose the chair across from where Slade sat. "Thought you could use a change in company for a couple of hours."

"Why would you think that?" Shadow looked to him before shrugging a shoulder with an overzealous smile. "We've been getting along splendidly. Haven't we, Digger?"

Digger.

She'd only referred to him as that since the night they'd almost crossed the line between co-workers and lovers. And though he'd been the one keeping her at arm's length ever since, Slade would give anything to hear his given name fall from her lips again.

"Yep."

He took a big bite of his sandwich, chewing and swallowing his food completely before opening the water Falcon had just slid his way. As he tilted his head back to accommodate a long, big gulp, he did everything in his power not to look the sexy blonde's way.

Slade wasn't trying to be an asshole, but he also couldn't afford to let himself become lost in her gaze. Because if their eyes met for more than a few seconds at a time, he feared he'd never again be able to look away.

"Okay, then," Bones responded as his attention bounced back and forth between Shadow and Slade. "That's…good. Great. Glad to hear it."

The other man's words and tone were both hesitant in nature, as if he didn't quit believe their corroborating claims.

"Did you guys just come here for lunch and conversation, or did you find out something new we can use to take down Senator Stanton?" Shadow asked.

"We're still working on it," Falcon told her.

The disappointment Slade caught from the corner of his eye reached into his chest and grabbed hold of his tightly guarded heart.

"So that would be a no," she guessed.

Bones' empathetic eyes softened at her obvious frustration. "Don't worry, Shadow. Trust me, I get how hard the waiting can be." He looked over at Falcon who was nodding his head. "We both do. But if we're going to go after the bastard, we have to be patient and smart."

"He's right," Slade supported his teammate, forcing himself to look Shadow's way. "If we want to take him down, we have to do it the right way."

"It's been twenty-six years," the brilliant woman bit back. "I think I've been patient long enough."

"You only just figured out it was him a few weeks ago," he quickly argued her point.

Totally misunderstanding the meaning behind his words, she abandoned her sandwich and rose to her feet.

"Right. Because if I'd remembered sooner, maybe he wouldn't be walking around a free man. Is that it?"

What?

"No." Slade gave a vehement shake of his head. "That's not at all what I was trying to—"

"Thanks for the food you guys." She turned her troubled gaze first to Bones and then to Falcon as she gave a quick lick of her lips. "But I'm not really all that hungry anymore."

"Ah, come on, Shadow." Bones did his best to appease her. "Don't be like that."

"I'm not trying to be like anything. I just…" She gave a quick shake of her head. "I didn't sleep all that well last night, and I think a nap would do me some good."

Shadow's claim of being tired was just an excuse to put some distance between herself and him. Slade knew this to the depth of his bones, and yet when the clearly frustrated woman left the table and started making her way back up the stairs, he didn't say or do a single thing to stop her.

"Well, then." Bones fell back in his chair. "That didn't exactly go as planned."

"She's just stressed." Slade heard himself making an excuse for a woman who'd rather hide away in her room rather than stay in the same room as him.

"Can't say that I blame her," Falcon muttered low. "Poor woman loses her mom as a kid and nearly three decades later discovers the man who killed her might be our country's next leader. That would be a tough pill for anyone to stomach."

Running a hand over his jaw, Slade used it to hide the way his teeth were clenching tightly together. Dammit, the last thing he wanted to do was upset her. He sure as shit didn't want her thinking he blamed her for letting a killer get away.

"Yeah, I don't know." Bones frowned, his knowing eyes searching Slade's a little too closely. "I mean, I get that we've only recently met her in person, but we've known that woman a good, long while." The man's southern drawl grew thicker with every new word. "She's gotten us through some pretty hairy situations, and never once have I ever heard her jump that quick to anger."

When his gaze narrowed with a hint of suspicion, Slade's defenses immediately rose.

"What the hell are you looking at me for?" He shot his teammate a deep scowl.

But Bones simply lifted one shoulder in a casual shrug.

"You tell me," the other man instructed. "You're the one who's been locked away with her the last few days. And, correct me if I'm wrong, but there seemed to be a healthy dose of tension in the air between you two. I don't suppose anything has…happened with you guys. Has it?"

"What did you just ask me?"

Keep your cool, Garrison. Keep your fucking cool.

"Easy, Dig." Bones lifted a defensive palm. "There's no judgment here. Good lookin' guy like yourself trapped here with a beautiful, funny, intelligent woman like Shadow…" He let his words trail. "Lord knows it wouldn't be the first time a member of Tac-Ops mixed business with pleasure."

"There's nothing going on between me and Shadow," he vowed. Technically, it was true despite how much he wished it wasn't.

"So you two haven't—"

"No." Slade's throat worked a swallow. "We haven't. Not that it would be any of your fucking business if we had."

Falcon chose that moment to jump back into the conversation. "I think what our well-meaning friend is trying to say is that if this…arrangement isn't working, one of us can spot you and stay with Shadow instead."

Like hell, you will.

I don't need a fucking spotter." He made that point crystal clear. Turning his full attention back to

Bones, Slade added, "And whatever you're thinking about me and her…don't. I'm here to do a job and nothing else. Got it?"

Bones waited a beat before raising both of his hands as a show of defeat. "If you say so."

"I do."

"Okay, then."

The silence that followed was rigid at best, but a few seconds later, Falcon quickly—and thankfully—changed the subject.

"Owens said to tell you he spoke with his most trusted contact within the CIA. Apparently that guy's getting Owens everything he can find on Stanton's time with the Agency."

Slade huffed out a breath. "That's all well and good, but I don't see how a bunch of redacted case files and reports are going to help us with—"

"We have to go!" Shadow's frantic voice sounded from the top of the stairs.

All three men swung their gazes her way, and when Slade saw the look on her face, his stomach filled with a strong sense of dread.

"What is it?" Slade shot to his feet, his chair nearly toppling over backward in the process.

He rushed her way as she ran down the stairs, Bones and Falcon falling right in line behind him.

"Ashley just called." She referred to their office manager as a well of unshed tears covered the blues of her eyes. "She said my dad's in the emergency room at Atrium Health Mercy. She said…she said he collapsed during a meeting with a client."

That dread he'd been feeling churned into full-blown concern

"Rafe?" Bones came to his side. "What the hell happened?"

"Ashley said the paramedics think it's a heart attack. She said they had to…" Her voice cracked preventing the rest of what she was going to say from coming out.

"Had to what?" he asked as he and the others followed her to the cabin's front door.

The woman who had him tied up in all sorts of knots turned her frantic gaze his way, and when she did, her chin began to quiver. "They had to shock him, Slade." Shadow had never sounded so small. "She said he went into v tach shortly after the ambulance got there, so they had to…oh, God. What if he—"

"He won't," Slade promised despite having no control whatsoever when it came to his boss's fate. But the woman was on the brink of falling apart and…selfishly…that was something he didn't think he could bear to see.

"You said Ashley told you they took him to Mercy?" Falcon double-checked on their way out the door.

Shadow's long ponytail bounced up and down as

she nodded, her short legs working overtime as she practically ran down the porch steps.

"We'll follow you there," Bones announced, the four of them splitting off to their respective rides.

The first several miles of the drive passed by in relative silence. When Slade did speak, it was to offer the woman next to him lame platitudes and more empty promises he couldn't guarantee.

To her credit, Shadow never fully broke down or told him to take a flying leap. The truth was, Slade would have welcomed that far more than the stark silence coming from the passenger seat.

"He'll be okay, Shadow," Slade told her again after more miles passed without a single shared word between them.

When she didn't respond, he found himself reaching a hand across the console to cover her knitted fists twisting together in her lap. Her movements froze, and for a moment, he thought he'd made yet another mistake where the amazing woman was concerned. But then she slowly turned one of her hands palm-up and linked her fingers with his.

"I can't lose him, Slade." Her voice was soft and filled with a worry he'd do anything to take away. "He's the only family I have. If I lose him, there won't be anyone left."

"You're wrong." He gave her hand a comforting squeeze. "We may not be blood, but me and the team…we're your family, too, sweetheart. And we're not going anywhere. No matter what."

* * *

SHADOW RACED into the emergency room entrance at Atrium Health Mercy. She didn't stop until she was standing in front of the intake desk connected to the ER's main lobby.

"Rafe Owens," she blurted her father's name as if that explained everything.

The nurse behind the desk glanced up from her computer monitor and smiled. "Hi, can I help you?"

"Rafe Owens," she bit out the repeated name, barely holding on to the last strings of her patience. "He's my father. I got a call he was brought here with a suspected heart attack."

Between the unending tension that had been present since that confusing night with Slade, the mess with Stanton, and now this…

A woman can only take so much before she loses her shit and goes full-on postal.

"Let me see which room they're treating him in." The young nurse's fingers began to fly over her keyboard. "You said the name was Owens?"

"Yes." Shadow spelled out both her father's first and last names.

The other woman frowned. "I'm sorry, but I'm not seeing him in our system."

"What do you mean he's not in your system? He was just brought here by ambulance less an hour ago."

"Maybe it's a glitch in the system," the well-meaning nurse offered. "Let me check again." A few seconds later, she shook her head, the look of sympathy in her eyes making Shadow want to scream. "I'm sorry, but there's no record of a Rafe Owens being brought here. Are you sure this is the right hospital?"

"Yes, I'm sure!" She turned to Slade who hadn't left her side. "Ashely told me it was here. She specifically said Atrium Health Mercy."

"Is there any way you can check to see if he's at another Atrium hospital?" Bones chimed in with a belatedly added, "Just in case Ashely was mistaken."

There were several Atrium medical facilities scattered in and around Charlotte, so maybe Ashely *had* gotten it wrong. Maybe the ambulance took him to one of them, instead.

But with the next shake of the nurse's head and the regret filling the woman's brown eyes, Shadow knew the answer before she parted her full, pink lips.

"I'm sorry, but that name isn't showing up anywhere in our system. I wish there were something more I could do to help."

Shadow's heart dropped into her churning stomach as she and the guys stepped out of the way of another incoming patient.

"This is ridiculous." She shoved her hand into her pocket and pulled out her cell. "I'm calling Ashley. Hopefully she can straighten this whole thing out."

But before she could even unlock her phone, Falcon had already beaten her to the punch.

"Hey, Ash, it's Garrett." Falcon held his own phone out, putting the call on speaker for them all to hear.

"Hey, Garrett," Ashley greeted him with her usual, friendly charm. "What's up?"

Shadow frowned at the other woman's casual tone.

What's up? Seriously?

They weren't calling to have a chat about the freaking weather. This was her father they were talking about. And as of right now, the man was MIA.

"We're at Atrium Mercy," Falcon responded in a rush. "We left the safe house to come straight here right after you called Shadow, but they're saying Owens isn't here."

"Mercy?" Ashley sounded genuinely confused. "What are you talking about?"

Shadow quickly inserted herself into the confusing conversation. "When you called me, you said the ambulance took Rafe to Atrium Mercy. But we're here, and they're telling us he's not—"

"I never called you, Shadow." The other woman's tone did a full one-eighty, going from friendly to serious in the blink of an eye. "I'm not sure what's happening, but you and I haven't spoken today, and Mr. Owens is in the conference room right now, meeting with a client."

"You're sure he's there?" Bones asked, his face twisted with the same look of confusion Shadow knew matched her own.

"I took him and the other gentleman a fresh carafe of coffee two minutes before you called, so… yeah. I'm pretty sure."

A wave of relief left Shadow's knees feeling weak, but then the reality of what had happened fully sank in. "Someone cloned Ashely's voice." Her eyes flew to the man standing to her immediate right. "Whoever it was got access to my phone number, and then they disguised their voice to make it sound exactly like Ashley's. And they know…" Her throat worked a painful swallow before she cleared it and tried again. "They know I'm Owens' daughter."

"Stanton," Digger rumbled the name as if it were a curse. "It has to be him."

"But why?"

"To force you out of hiding," Bones answered somberly. He started looking around, as if he expected the murdering son of a bitch to appear right there, in the middle of the emergency room lobby.

"He's right." Digger put a protective hand to her lower back and began guiding her toward the exit. "We need to get you the hell out of here. Now."

"And go where?" Shadow's steps quickened to

keep up. "If they accessed my phone, then they probably know where the cabin is."

"Good point." He didn't miss a beat as he grabbed the device still clutched in her hand.

The second they stepped through the automatic doors, he dropped it onto the concrete below. And then, he stomped his booted heel down hard in the center of its screen.

A spiderweb of cracks appeared as the glass broke beneath the weight of his foot. Digger bent down, scooped up the phone, and then he used both hands to nearly break the thing fully in half.

He tossed the destroyed device in the trash. "I'll buy you a new one," he offered with a low, angry mutter. Slade took her hand in his and began leading her to his car.

All three men kept their heads moving in constant swivels as they walked. Shadow, too, because the threat could come at them from anywhere at any time.

And because she hadn't questioned the validity of what she now assumed was an AI-generated call, they'd walked themselves right into a killer's trap.

Their cars were parked next to the no-parking curb about twenty yards from the emergency room entrance. As they marched down the long sidewalk toward the two vehicles, Digger used his free hand to retrieve his keys from his pocket.

"So what's the plan?" Bones asked from a few steps back.

"I'm taking her to the office," he announced curtly. "We'll talk with Owens and decide our next steps from there."

"Sounds good," Falcon agreed. "We'll be right behind you."

Shadow remained quiet, her thoughts running in twelve different directions. She was relieved beyond words to know her father was okay. But on the flip side of that, she was positively *livid* knowing she'd fallen for Stanton's obvious trick to bring her back out into his sights.

Her steps quickened even more, and soon she was inching her way into the lead. Keeping a protective hold on her hand, Digger lifted his other to point the fob toward the spot where he'd parked. He pressed the button to remotely start the vehicle's engine, and then—

The air around her erupted into a giant ball of flames.

Shadow felt herself being lifted off her feet as she was thrown backward through the air. Though she tried to hold on, her hand was ripped from Digger's with an unstoppable force.

She was tossed into a nearby patch of manicured grass, her body landing hard against the unforgiving ground. A flash of pain struck as her head bounced with what felt like a crushing blow, and she thought she may have heard Digger call out her name.

But then the darkness prevailed, and her eyes fell shut. And after that, there was…

Nothing.

CHAPTER 9

"I'M FINE."

Slade's infuriated gaze remained locked on the frowning woman sitting up on the gurney. Rage and fear still ran strong through the hard thumping of his heart, leaving his hands in white-knuckled fists at his sides.

"You're not fine," he growled.

Yes, he fucking *growled.* And no, he didn't care.

Someone had placed an incendiary device on his car with the hopes that he and Shadow would be inside it when it blew. They'd come close to succeeding. Too damn close.

And if he'd pressed the button on his key fob a few seconds later…

We'd both be dead.

Slade had come to grips with the idea of death years ago. He wasn't afraid to die and some days even welcomed the idea. No, the murderous inferno raging inside had nothing to do with his own mortality and everything to do with the woman he was supposed to protect.

"I have a headache and some bruises," Shadow argued as she moved her head to the side in an effort to avoid the nurse's hands.

"You have a concussion and a cut on your scalp that this nurse is *trying* to butterfly shut." Taking a step closer, he put his hands on his hips and shot her a pointed stare.

"Just slap a band aid on it and call it good." She scowled. "I need to see my dad."

"Owens is fine," Digger assured her. "I told you earlier, I spoke to him on the phone while you were off getting your CT."

"Yeah, well I was sure that was Ashley who called me earlier, too. Look how that turned out."

"That's why I used FaceTime when I called," he countered.

"All done." The kind nurse smiled as she finished placing the small, white strips over the cut near her patient's bloodied hairline.

"So that's it?" Shadow shot the other woman a hopeful glance. "I can leave?"

"I'll go get your discharge papers from the doctor now."

She wasn't gone two seconds before the stubborn

blonde swung her legs off the portable bed. But when Shadow stood a little too quickly, she started to sway.

A deep curse flew out from under Slade's breath as he shoved his way past Bones on his way over to her side. With his hands on her shoulders, he kept her steady as she held onto the lowered bedrail and closed her eyes.

"Easy, dammit." He admonished her for not waiting until someone could help. "You need to slow the hell down and take a breath before you wind up hurting yourself more than you already are."

With her head still down and her eyes remaining closed, Shadow grimaced as she kept a tight grip on the plastic railing. "Good thing you don't have to worry about patient satisfactory scores, because your bedside manner really sucks."

Bones snorted with a chuckle from a few feet back. "And this surprises you how exactly?"

"Oh, I'm not surprised." The stubborn woman peeled her lids open and glanced his way. "Just pointing out the obvious."

"Damn, brother. She's got you pegged." Then to Shadow, Bones said, "Honestly, I'm shocked you haven't killed him by now after being locked away with him in that cabin for the last few days."

Slade's jaw muscles flexed with the clenching of his teeth. If he wasn't so damn happy Bones and Falcon came away from the blast with little more than a few scratches, he'd be tempted to shoot the comedic medic, himself.

"You're right." He ignored his teammate's comments, focusing solely on Shadow. "I don't give a shit about satisfaction scores, and I don't care if my tone offends you. It's my job to *protect* you, and that's what I'm trying to do. But you—"

"What? Almost ruined your perfect record?" she seethed, the blues of her eyes darkening with anger and some other emotion he couldn't quite decipher.

"My what?"

"You know…the *record*."

Slade blinked when she failed to offer anything more. "You keep saying that as if I know what the hell you're talking about."

"She's talking about the fact that, to date, no one on Tac-Ops has ever lost a client we've been hired to protect." Bones took it upon himself to explain. To Shadow, the other man added, "But technically, you didn't hire us either, so…I'm thinking this may not actually count toward the record."

That's what she thought he was upset about?

Slade grew silent, letting his arms drop down to his sides as he took a step back to give her some room. "We should go." His tone sounded flatter than normal, even to his own ears. "If you're still hell bent on leaving, we need to get you to the office. You can see your dad, and then I'll take you someplace safe."

"Do you know where?"

"Not yet, but we have to assume the cabin's been burned, and your father agrees. He already has a clean-up crew headed out there to grab our things and erase any evidence we were ever there."

A look of sadness flashed before she blinked it away. As for Slade, he was fine never going back. He'd never admit it, of course, but every time he'd step foot in the cabin's entrance or inadvertently caught a glimpse of her bed through her room's opened door, he'd remember.

The kissing. The touching. That brief moment in time when he'd lost himself in her arms.

It was both Heaven and Hell being there with her and not giving in to his deepest desires. So while he hated the reason, Slade couldn't help but think a change of scenery would do them both some good.

With any luck, it would help remind him that this was nothing more than another job. That Shadow was no different than any other woman he and his teammates had been assigned to protect in the past.

Yeah, you tell yourself that bullshit enough times, Garrison, and you might actually start to believe it.

Probably not, but you couldn't blame a guy for trying.

The nurse from before returned with discharge papers in hand, and a few short minutes later, they were walking out the door.

"Owens sent over another car, since yours and the one we were driving both got destroyed in the blast,"

Falcon informed the group as a whole. "There should also be a couple of uniformed officers waiting to escort us to the office, just in case."

Sure enough, as they stepped outside, Slade saw one of Tac-Ops' blacked-out SUV's ready and waiting. Just as Falcon had claimed, there was also a marked Charlotte PD cruiser parked in front, as well as another one waiting to follow their replacement SUV from behind.

"It never ceases to amaze me how much pull my father actually has," Shadow muttered as a man Slade recognized as one of Owens' trusted drivers opened the back passenger door.

The guy stood silently off to the side and waited as she carefully climbed inside.

Slade followed suit, sliding himself onto the bench seat next to where she sat. Falcon took the front while Bones went around to the other side. With Shadow sandwiched between him and Bones, Slade gave their driver a nod, letting him know they were ready to roll.

They rode back to the office in silence, Slade and the others each lost in their own thoughts. Though he tried like hell not to let himself go there, his mind kept replaying the terrifying scene over and over again in his head.

Like Shadow, he'd been pissed as hell for having fallen for what they now knew was a trap meant to end both their lives. Then he'd pushed that damn button, sending them all flying in different directions.

He could still see her lying in the grass, bleeding and far too still. Slade had gone crazy, then, nearly falling back down to his ass as he'd scrambled his way over to her. He'd never felt such an overwhelming sense of relief as he had when she'd opened those gorgeous blue eyes.

I could have killed her.

A few more seconds, and that's exactly what would have happened. And that knowledge—and the images that came with it—was something that would haunt him for the rest of his days.

"Hey, Dig." Bones' voice cut through his torturous thoughts, pulling him back into the present. "We're here."

Slade blinked and looked out his window to find they were already stopped inside their building's secured garage. The underground space was kept safe by an armed guard posted by its gate, and the elevator a few yards from where they sat would take them straight up to the building's top floor.

Once there, the four of them walked the few feet down the hallway to the official Tac-Ops office. A distraught looking Ashley was at the door, waiting when they arrived.

"I am so sorry, Shadow," the young woman apologized the second they made their way inside. "I don't know how someone managed to not only clone the office number but also mask their voice so it sounded exactly like mine."

"It's not your fault," Shadow offered, sounding sincere in both her words and tone. "With technology what it is today, all it takes is the knowledge and the right equipment. And sometimes, a little luck. But yeah…generative AI is getting more and more accurate by the day. It's terrifying, actually."

"Tell me about it." Ashley's round eyes grew with a nod. "I still don't understand how they even got your private number, let alone my voice."

"The person we're dealing with is former deep-work CIA," Bones told her. "There's not a lot those guys *can't* do."

"He's right." Owens appeared from the hallway that led to their individual offices and the Tac-Ops conference room. "If this *was* Stanton, and it's looking more and more like it is, then for him, pulling off something like this would be like child's play."

Shadow didn't say a word on her way to Owens. And when she got to her father, she moved seamlessly into the man's muscular arms.

"I was so worried about you." She spoke softly, clearly not caring that she had an audience of four.

"You took the words right out of my mouth." The seasoned operative closed his eyes and kissed the top of her head. "I was halfway to the parking garage before Digger finally convinced me to remain here, rather than racing over to the hospital where you were."

Pulling free from her father's embrace, Shadow

gave Slade a quick glance before turning back with a slight nod. "We didn't want to risk the same thing happening to you."

"Speaking of which…" Falcon took a step forward, sliding his hands into the front pockets of his jeans. "We need to check over every vehicle in that garage." His eyes locked onto their boss. "Starting with yours."

"Already done," Owens informed them. "While you were finishing up at the hospital, I had the entire place checked. No signs of explosives or trackers were found."

"Well, that's good, at least," Bones mumbled low before asking their boss, "So what now?"

"Now, we go over everything we know up to this point, and then we make a new plan. Apollo is already waiting for us in the conference room."

Slade and the others dipped their chins in agreement with their boss's agenda. Minutes later, they were sitting around the large conference room table, recounting the events leading up to the bombing.

"My contact within the CIA has confirmed what we already suspected to be true," Owens began. "My late wife, Shadow's mother, did wet work for the CIA."

"She was a government assassin," Shadow clarified with a shrug. "Might as well call it like it is."

"Very well." Owens conceded to his daughter's request. "Amanda was a government assassin, as was her partner, Michael Stanton. At the time of her death, my wife and Stanton were working under the guise of being attorneys who worked together at a law firm in Columbus. While they were both legitimately licensed to practice law in the state of Ohio, their primary job was to take out targets the agency deemed as national, and sometimes global, threats."

"Why would Stanton want to kill his partner?" Apollo asked from his usual seat across the table from Slade.

"That's a very good question." Their boss sighed. "Unfortunately, that's information I have yet to uncover."

"What does your contact think?" Shadow asked. "Has he said whether the hit on Mom was sanctioned?"

"He's still looking into it. So far, he's found no evidence tying your mother's death to anything official."

"Yeah, but off-the-books jobs happen every day," Falcon countered. "Just because there isn't a record of an official order being given doesn't mean it didn't happen."

"I agree." Owens nodded. "Which is why my man on the inside is still digging."

"What if it wasn't an ordered hit?" Shadow pondered aloud. "What if Mom did some digging on her own, and what she uncovered got her killed?"

"You think she had something on Stanton?" Slade asked.

Her blue eyes turned his way. "It's the only alternative that makes any sense."

"He's dirty, she finds out, maybe threatens to expose him…" Apollo nodded. "Definitely plausible. It would also explain why he's so concerned about Shadow ousting him as her mother's killer."

"Apollo makes a good point," Owens addressed the group as a whole. "Redacted or not, if the hit *was* sanctioned, there would be some sort of paper trail linking Stanton's unit to the job."

"One lone gunman blasting a motel room with bullets from across a parking lot doesn't exactly scream spy job to me," Digger agreed before turning to Shadow. "But didn't you say Stanton has a rock-solid alibi for the night of your mother's murder?"

The slight snorting sound coming from the mildly concussed woman eased some of the tension still holding his muscles hostage.

"The guy's wife told police he was home all night with her and their son. They had dinner together as a family, and after their son fell asleep, they stayed up half the night watching movies from their couch. Security footage doesn't show anyone going in or out of the residence, but you and I both know technology can be manipulated to fit whatever narrative a person wants to spin."

"Okay, so going back to the working theory that

Stanton was a dirty agent…" Bones straightened his spine. "If your wife somehow did find out whatever the guy was up to, killing her makes total sense."

Piggybacking off of that, Falcon added, "It also explains why the guy wouldn't want his time with the Agency exposed to the public. He's already spent millions of his own money trying to smooth-talk his way into the Oval Office."

"Nothing brings out the worst in people like a threat to their money and freedom," Shadow glanced around the room. Clarity filled her gorgeous, tormented gaze when she turned her focus back onto Slade. "We need to go on the offensive. If we can find out what my mom had on Stanton, we can use it to take him down once and for all."

"That sound's all well and good…" Apollo rejoined the conversation. "But how do we do that when the prick's history with the CIA has been completely erased?"

"We don't need the CIA's records. We just need to find the person who tried blowing us up. And *that* starts with me checking out the feed from the hospital's security cameras."

"You think whoever put the explosives on Dig's car was careless enough to get caught on camera?" Bones asked next.

Shadow merely shrugged, looking and sounding more and more like her old self with each second that passed.

"It's worth a shot," she told their team's medic. "I mean, they were stupid enough to try to blow us up in broad daylight surrounded by witnesses, right? And as my father so astutely pointed out, whoever turned my motel room into Swiss cheese didn't do so with the usual stealth of a government hitman."

Not waiting for a response, she carefully pushed herself to her feet.

A renewed sense of rage toward the person who'd tried to kill her began to swirl around in Slade's gut, but then he saw the strength and determination present in her fiery gaze. He couldn't deny the sense of pride he felt knowing the two recent attempts on her life hadn't broken her in the least.

If anything, the incredible woman seemed even more resolved in her pursuit of justice. And despite the fear that Stanton wouldn't stop in his efforts to silence her forever, Shadow's unwillingness to give up made him like her even more.

Easy, Garrison. You keep going down that path, you could end up doing a whole lot more than just liking her. If you're not careful, you just might find yourself falling in—

"We can do that from the safe house." Slade cleared his throat and rose quickly to his feet, doing his damnedest to ignore the thought trying to drive itself into his head.

Her confused stare found him once again. "I thought you said we weren't going back to the cabin."

"You aren't," Owens answered for him. "I had

your things taken to a different location. One here in the city." The gray-haired man turned to his daughter, who was still standing beside her pushed-in chair. "I decided it was best to keep you closer. And now that we know he isn't above using our relationship to his favor, you will remain in the new safe house until he's either behind bars or dead."

"That could take months, if it ever happens at all," the man's daughter argued. "I'm not going to let this guy dictate how I live my life."

"And I'm not going to let him *take* your life." Emotion poured into Owens' concerned gaze. "I already lost your mother to this son of a bitch. I'm not about to lose you, too."

The room grew quiet as Shadow worked her throat with an audible swallow. "What about you?" she asked her father quietly. "Stanton may not have come after you this time, but that doesn't mean he won't."

"The guys and I can stay with you, Boss," Falcon offered. "Just in case."

"Party at the boss's house." Bones grinned with a playful nod. "What could go wrong?"

In response to this, Owens countered with a serious, "Two of you can stay with me at the plantation, but I want one of you to watch over Ashley, as well. Stanton pulled her into this the second he used the likeness of her voice to trick Shadow into coming out of hiding. There's no reason to think the bastard isn't above actually going after Ashley."

"Good idea." Shadow nodded. "Oh, and Dig said you had our things brought here from the cabin?"

"Not here," her father clarified. "It's already at the new safe house."

The tempting blonde turned Slade's way next. "I say we get to wherever it is we're going. Sooner we get there, the sooner I can get to work on the footage from the hospital."

Just like that, she was back to being mission ready. As for Slade, he began to wonder if perhaps, deep down, he was a closeted masochist. Because a part of him—a big part, if he were being completely honest—was suddenly looking forward to it being just the two of them again.

CHAPTER 10

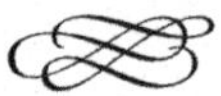

Two hours later...

"I'm in." Shadow blew out a breath of relief when the new window popped up on her laptop's screen.

"Good." Digger's deep voice traveled through the otherwise still air. Grumbled one-word responses were pretty much all he'd offered since leaving the hospital to come here.

Their newest home away from home was a high-end apartment in the heart of downtown Charlotte. And regardless of her feelings about being sequestered away, she couldn't deny this place was even nicer than the cabin in the woods.

When it came to safe houses, her father apparently spared no expense. But the two spaces he'd utilized couldn't be any more different.

The cabin had been an impressive display of rich, rustic charm, whereas the space in which she and Digger were holed up now was a modern creation of white walls and accents of black and gray. The two safe houses were opposite in almost every single way, much like her and Digger.

Speaking of Dig…

Shadow stole a glimpse of the tall, dark, and ridiculously handsome man from over the top of her screen. His broad back was to her as he looked through the sliding glass doors leading to the apartment's private, fifth-floor balcony. He'd been even quieter than usual since leaving the Tac-Ops office, which for him, was saying a heck of a lot.

When she'd first regained consciousness after nearly getting her ass blown to smithereens, she'd found him staring down at her through a sea of tumultuous emotion. And, apart from when medical staff had taken her away for the doctor ordered CT, Slade had stayed right by her side the entire time, refusing to let a doctor check him out, as well.

To be fair, he seemed physically okay, save a few scratches and scrapes and a bruise on his left cheek. Shadow had done what she could to convince him to let a doctor do a quick once-over, but he'd instantly—and vehemently—declined. He'd told her his only concern was knowing she was okay.

That, of course, was incredibly sweet, and made her like the big jerk even more than she already did.

Which sucked because Digger had made himself pretty clear about where the two of them stood. And it wasn't anywhere near where Shadow wanted them to be.

That's a different problem for a different day.

She blinked away her wandering thoughts because her inner voice was right. There was a much more pressing matter that needed her undivided attention, so she put aside her feelings for the stubborn, stoic man and chose to return her focus on stopping a killer.

"The hospital's security system isn't all that impressive," Shadow kept the topic of conversation to the task at hand and nothing else. "Now we just have to cross our fingers and pray I got to the footage before Stanton's minions."

She looked back at the screen and began rewinding from the present back to just before she and the rest of the team arrived. A few minutes into the search, she saw Digger's car racing to a stop near the emergency room's entrance. Right behind it was the SUV that had been carrying Falcon and Bones.

Feeling as though she were watching some sort of bizarre movie starring her and her friends, Shadow observed herself practically jump out of Digger's passenger seat before he'd fully brought the vehicle to a complete stop.

Her chest tightened when she caught sight of her recorded image's worried expression. The panic she'd felt while running through those doors still so close to the surface, it would take no effort at all to conjure it back to life.

He's okay. Dad's alive and well, and he's totally okay.

It was the same mental reminder she'd given herself since seeing her father at the office following the explosion.

He was okay, as were Digger, Bones, and Falcon. They were all still alive, and minus some minor injuries, they were all okay.

But they almost weren't, and she was the reason for that. It was her fault Digger and their other two teammates almost died. Now her father and poor Ashley had been dragged into her mess, and she couldn't manage to find a shred of evidence linking Stanton to any of his crimes.

There!

Movement behind Digger's car caught Shadow's attention, and she hurried to rewind the footage. Her gaze narrowed as it became even more focused than before, and she tapped a few keys to change the recording to play in half-time speed.

She watched and waited, not daring to take her eyes off the small screen for even a second. A man appeared from the bottom left corner, as if he'd just come out the lobby's automatic doors. He was wearing a black ball cap with the bill pulled down tight, a matching jacket, pants, and a pair of lace-up boots.

Shadow watched as he walked approached Digger's car using slow, casual steps. His hands were in the pockets of his jacket, and for a moment, she thought she'd made a mistake. But then…

Bingo.

Her eyes followed the man's every move, including the way he was subtly inching closer to the side of Digger's car. He stepped off the curb to walk between the back of the car and the team's front bumper.

Shadow's chest grew tight, her stomach churning with anger when she saw what the man did next. It happened so quickly she almost missed it.

Lucky for her, she didn't.

The man moved to walk between the two vehicles, pulling something small and square out of his right pocket. Seconds before he moved between the two vehicles, he reached out and placed what had to be the bomb beneath the edge of Digger's rear bumper.

Son of a…

"I've got him!" Shadow blurted out excitedly, rushing to rewind the video back several seconds. Then she watched that part over again.

"Are you sure?" Digger marched toward her from where he'd been standing across the room.

Using the coffee table as a desk, she remained on the couch, spinning the laptop around so the screen was facing him. "You tell me."

He stopped, his eyes immediately going to the

frozen image. Leaning in, his gaze narrowed slightly as if to better focus on what he was seeing.

The muscles at the side of his bearded jaw twitched, and his hardened expression practically turned to stone.

"Can you get facial rec?"

She spun the computer back around, her hands immediately going to the keys. She typed and talked, giving him the best answer she had.

"The angle isn't great, and the bastard purposely kept his hat down low to avoid being seen on the footage. I'll have to play around with it a bit to try to get the clearest shot of his face."

"How long until you know?"

"Hard to say. If I can't get a clean image from this camera, which it's looking like that's going to be the case, then I'll have to see if I can find him in the footage from one of the others. Why?" She sent a quick smirk in his direction. "You got someplace else you need to be?"

"Just the shower."

Shadow's fingers froze, their tips hovering a few centimeters above the keyboard. Unwanted images of Digger naked and wet filled her mind's eye in a flash.

Nope, nope, nope. You cannot think about that now. There's a man out there who tried blowing the both of you up today. Find him, stop Stanton, and then maybe…

"You have time." She brought her focus back down to the screen.

Digger didn't say anything more, but he also didn't immediately leave. He just stood there, a few feet from where she sat working, not talking or moving or doing anything other than staring. Until finally, blessedly, he turned and walked away.

Shadow refused to look, knowing if she did she'd once again become distracted. She'd stolen enough glances over the last few days to know he was a weakness she couldn't afford.

The sound of running water reached her ears minutes later. A stretch of time passed, and at first, she thought she'd finally become a master at Operation Ignore How Sinfully Sexy Digger Is.

A few seconds later, the tempting images returned in full force, and no matter how hard she tried, she could think of nothing but him.

"GAH!" Shadow released a frustrating growl as she shot up from the couch and grabbed her computer with a huff.

Biting back the creative string of curse words close to the tip of her tongue, she stormed out of the living room and through the sliding glass doors. She slammed it shut behind her, using much more force than necessary.

Shadow stopped and looked around, spotting a small patio table and two chairs positioned against the balcony's back corner several feet to her left. She walked over and set her laptop onto the rounded glass before plopping down into the chair with its back nearly touching the building's brick wall.

The air was warm and a touch thicker than she preferred, but she pulled as much of it as she could into her lungs, holding it there a few seconds longer, before releasing it back into the wild.

Boy, what a mess her life had become, and she had no one to blame but herself. That wasn't true. Michael Stanton was really the one to blame. She just prayed that she and the team could find their smoking gun soon…before it was too late.

SLADE STEPPED out of the shower and onto the plush white mat covering the tiled floor. His bare feet sank deep as he reached for the nearby towel he'd hung up on the hook to his right. He was halfway through drying off his legs when the sound of a door slamming shut sounded from the floor below.

He stood tall, his spine becoming stiff with the tensing of his muscles. Wrapping the towel around his waist, he ignored the drips of water still present on his dampened skin as he exited the humid space and made his way across the bedroom.

Once there, he reached out, opening the door and peeking his head through the opening into the hall.

"Shadow?" Slade called out for her.

Silence was his only response.

Moving fully into the hallway, he walked a few feet to his left, stopping midway between his bedroom door and the top of the apartment's split-level stairs. He looked over the black metal railing to his right, but Shadow was no longer sitting on the couch where he'd left her. And her computer was also missing from the glass coffee table.

Slade turned and went back the way he'd come. Bypassing the room that would be his for the foreseeable future, he continued down the hall to the next door on the right.

He knocked, and the door moved slowly beneath the force of his hand. Once again, he called out for the woman he'd been assigned to protect, and once again, she didn't call back.

After letting himself in to double-check that her bedroom and bathroom were both void of her presence, Slade checked the other spare room and bathroom on the second level. With no sign of Shadow being on the second floor, he picked up his pace and hurried toward the stairs.

His hand held the knotted towel at his hip to keep the damn thing from coming loose and falling to the floor. When he reached the bottom, he looked around, first in the half-bath on that level and then the open kitchen, which extended from the expansive living room.

Where are you?

Slade turned to his right, his gaze searching the part of the balcony he could see through the long, partially opened curtains. Doing his best to keep his burgeoning worry at bay, he went to the massive glass door and slid it open.

He didn't see her at first, and damn if a jolt of panic didn't start to set in. But then—

"I didn't realize the dress code was so relaxed around here."

Shadow's voice came from his left, and he swung his gaze that way. With her computer resting on the small patio table where she sat, she had her bare feet propped up on the empty chair to her right.

She was dressed in a pair of cotton shorts and a black tank that didn't quite cover her abs, and the tips of her long hair blew with the passing breeze. Her eyes met his, and there was a glimmer of humor there. One matching the ornery smirk lifting one corner of her tempting mouth.

Damn, she's beautiful.

"I called for you, but you didn't answer. Next time tell me before you come outside by yourself."

The gruff order sent her head back in a slight recoil, her big blue eyes blinking as she stared back at him with surprise. Not sounding apologetic in the least, she shot back with a sarcastic response.

"I'm sorry." Her words sounded about as disingenuous as her expression. "But as your current state of undress clearly reflects, you were otherwise indisposed."

"You could've hollered at me from the door."

"And miss all this?" She motioned toward his almost naked form.

On reflex, his fists slid a bit lower to help shield the erection starting to form beneath the terrycloth towel. "You know, I get that everything's a big fucking joke to you, but it's my job to protect you, and I can't exactly do that if I have no idea where you are."

"A job." Shadow snorted humorlessly, dropping her feet so she could stand. "Because that's all I am to you, right?" She picked up her computer, storming toward him along the balcony before going back inside.

Anger broiled just beneath the surface as he did his best not to let it run free.

"That's not what I meant, and you know it." Slade followed her in.

Her back remained to him as she marched angrily toward the kitchen. She set the laptop onto the island's gray and white granite countertop so hard, he was surprised it didn't break. While it continued to run whatever software system she had going, the scowling woman turned back around to face him.

"No, see, that's where you're wrong. I actually *don't* know that because you've pretty much stopped talking to me these past few days."

What the…

"I've talked to you."

"A grunt here or a couple of words there doesn't count, and you know it. Seriously tell me one meaningful conversation the two of us have shared." When Slade opened his mouth to remind her of how he'd told her about his mom, she shut him down with a clarifying, "And I'm talking about *after* the night you unilaterally decided there would never be an us."

His gut clenched and his chest grew tight as his lungs pulled in a sharp inhale. "I already explained that to you, Shadow. I'm not—"

"The man for me." She tossed his own words from that night right back in his face. "Yeah, I heard you loud and clear, big guy. But you see, I'm thinking that's not entirely true."

"What the hell do you mean, it's not true? You think I'm lying?"

I'd never lie to you.

"Not a lie, exactly. More like an excuse to keep me or anyone else from getting too close to the real you."

The real…

"I don't pretend to be someone I'm not."

"No, you just don't think you deserve the same happiness the rest of us do. And I get it, Dig." Shadow released a sardonic chuckle. "Trust me, I'm the queen of self-deprecating. Why do you think I spent so much time on the computer as a child? I could make it do whatever I wanted. Be whoever I wanted to be. There was no judgement from other kids like I got at school. No field trips or class parties where everyone's mom showed up but mine. No one to point and whisper about the poor little girl who saw her mommy get shot in the head."

"You're more than that, and you know it."

"I do now. Or at least I'm starting to see it. But it's so obvious to me that *you* don't see *your* worth. It breaks my heart to know you don't believe you deserve the same happiness the other guys on the team have all found. To know that, deep down, you honestly don't think you deserve to be...loved. And before you get your panties in a twist, I'm not saying you and I are destined for forever. I'm just saying you should have that with *someone*, you know? Or at least give it a try. I mean...what's the worst that could happen?"

"The worst that could..." He shook his head as his face twisted into an incredulous stare. "You've *seen* the worst, Alice. You know exactly what happens to the women who end up with guys like us."

She blinked in what appeared to be a shocked reaction to hearing him say her real name for the very first time. But almost as quickly, a sad smile lifted the corners of Shadow's mouth as she took a few hesitant steps forward.

"You're right. I *have* seen what happened to them." Her gaze remained locked onto his as she listed off his teammates' women. "Avery, Nicki, Evie...I've seen all of their smiles and heard their laughter. I know all about the weddings I never attended and their promises of a future none of them can wait to fulfill."

"That's not what I—"

"I know what you meant," she interrupted him again. "And trust me, I get that I probably sound like the world's biggest hypocrite right now. It's just that… I don't know." Shadow blew out a frustrated breath. "I guess almost dying twice in less than a week has given me some perspective on a few things. Namely, I finally realized just how precious the time we have here really is. And I don't know about you, but I'm sick to death of wasting it. Because in case you hadn't noticed, that's what people like us do."

Slade remained quiet, his muscles unmoving as he processed everything he'd just heard. This woman—this incredible, frustrating, amazing woman—was actually mad that she couldn't see himself through her gorgeous eyes.

"We spend our lives keeping everyone at arm's length until one day we wake up and there's no one left to hold onto," Shadow continued. "And I want someone to hold onto, Dig. Even if it's only for a little while. It's taken me a long time to see it, but I finally realized I deserve at least that much. And whether you want to believe it, you do, too."

It made no sense that this woman saw him as someone so deserving.

The obstinate beauty knew him in action, first-hand. From behind her computer, she'd witnessed him as the hardened Tac-Ops team leader.

Shadow had listened through the team's comms as he'd taken multiple enemy lives. And despite all of that—and his less than sunny disposition—she'd still said all those wonderful things.

But what surprised him even more was the fact that Shadow genuinely seemed to *believe* them. And if he was being completely honest, as he stood there staring back at her, he had no idea what he was supposed to do with all of that.

You know exactly what you should do. You're just afraid you'll do something to screw it all up.

Slade locked eyes with the woman he was beginning to think was his personal savior, knowing they were opposites in about every way that mattered. But perhaps it was *because* of those same differences that they somehow made the perfectly imperfect pair.

He took a step toward her, first one and then another. Moving slowly, his eyes never once left hers. And when he was mere inches from where she stood, Slade stopped.

He didn't speak, because he was a man of action. In fact, Slade didn't utter a solitary sound. Instead he brought a hand to the unbruised side of her face. And when he leaned in close…he slammed his mouth to hers.

* * *

"ONE JOB." Doug Easton fumed at the man he'd trusted to get the job done. "You had *one* fucking job, and yet, she's still alive."

Andrew Reiner—a mid-level field agent Doug had easily blackmailed into doing his bidding—stared up at him with a guarded expression. "Like I told you on the phone, there was a problem with the device."

"A problem." Doug huffed out a breath with a disbelieving shake of his head.

"Yes, Easton. A problem." The shorter-than-average man glared. "Look, I get that it didn't go as planned but shit like this happens more than you think."

"Shit happens? That's all you have to say?"

"There's not much else I *can* say."

"You could tell me you have another way to eliminate the problem. Otherwise, I'll have to pay that pretty, unsuspecting wife of yours a visit to let her know her husband hasn't just lied to her about what he does for a living, but he's also been sleeping with another agent for the past six months."

Reiner's entire existence was filled with danger and death, yet the threat Doug had just laid down at the other man's feet created a visible flash of fear. A thin layer of visible threat beaded on the short bastard's forehead as he took an angry step forward.

"I told you I'd take care of it, and I will," he vowed. "In fact, if you'd given me time to talk, rather than barging in here with your admonishments and threats, I would have told you I already know exactly where the target is."

Doug's heart kicked hard with a hope he knew he shouldn't possess. "Where?"

"She and the guy who drove her to the hospital are staying at a high-end apartment downtown."

"How?"

"Why does it matter, how?"

"It was your job to kill her, and your last plan failed." He took a menacing step forward. "So I'll ask you one more time…how?"

The man's dark eyes didn't hide their own frustration as the muscles at the sides of his long jaw twitched. "Explosives are a tricky thing, so I always have a back-up in place. After the ill-timed explosion, I backtracked to the other side of the hospital, changed into the pair of scrubs I was wearing under my other clothes, and then I took the back way through the hospital and waltzed right into the E.R."

"Then what?"

"I waited." Reiner pulled a small tablet from the bag slung over one shoulder. "I knew our girl was knocked out by the blast, and typical concussion protocol would be a CT to also rule out a brain bleed. So I made myself scarce until the techs came down to get her, and I *accidentally* bumped into her gurney when they started pushing her down the hall."

The other man tapped the tablet's screen, flipping it around for Doug to see. He watched as the footage began to play, and within seconds, he realized what Reiner had done.

"You put a tracker on her shoe?"

"No one ever thinks to check the shoes." Reiner shrugged. "And before you bring it up, as far as the bombing is concerned, the cops won't be looking for a guy in scrubs. So I'm not concerned about having been seen inside the building. Hiding in plain sight and all that." He began tapping the tablet's screen once again. "Anyway"—the other man continued—"after our girl left here, she went to a high-rise downtown, where she remained for about an hour and a half. From there, the tracker shows her going to a new apartment building a few blocks away. Nice place, which means it has lots of security."

"You saying you can't get to her?"

"Not at all. Just that it's going to be a challenge. But, if you're willing to forgo discretion for effectiveness, I know a couple of guys willing to help. Best I've ever used, to tell you the truth. They don't ask questions, do exactly as they're told, and they'll take it to their graves." Reiner added a belated, "For the right price, of course."

The right price.

There was always a price. For Reiner's men, it was money. For Reiner, it was making sure his trusting wife never found out she'd married a liar and a cheat.

As for Doug, his price was a bit more complicated than that. He had plenty of money, no wife or kids, and no strings whatsoever. For him, it was about the love of the chase, and the thrills he got from the deadly risks he so willingly took.

And then there was Stanton. The man who relied on Doug far too often to clean up the messes the idiot inevitably made. But having a senator in his back pocket…or even better, the U.S. President, well…that was worth all the risks Doug had ever made combined.

Giving Reiner a stark warning, he told the man, "You have one chance to make this right, Andrew. But listen closely, because there's been a slight change of plans."

CHAPTER 11

FINALLY.

Shadow fell into Digger's arms, the front of her body pressing against his bare, sculpted chest. His hand slid from her cheek, his fingers gently finding their way up under her hair.

He was kissing her as if she might suddenly disappear. Thanks to Stanton, she almost had.

Digger's masculine groan of pleasure met her moan, vanquishing all thoughts of near-death experiences and killers. At five-three, she was a full foot shorter than the tall, dark, and fascinating man. So to avoid missing even an ounce of the pleasure his mouth was creating, she balanced on her tiptoes and cranked her neck back.

Hot. Wet. The kiss was erotic and all-consuming. And the way Slade was holding her body flush with his…

It's like we're two pieces of a perfect puzzle.

Shadow's nails dug into the skin at his back as she kept a tight grip on his broad shoulders. He was warm and slightly damp from his recent shower, his scent a mixture of soap and shampoo, along with his own natural, masculine spice.

Her mouth opened wider, letting more of him in as their tongues swirled and danced in an explosion of euphoric bliss. Digger swallowed her next moan as his hands slid low on her back, and her hips instinctively moved forward toward his.

Butterflies swirled when the impressive bulge between his toweled thighs pressed against her lower belly. Her sex filled with desire, and her inner muscles clenched with anticipation from the magic the two of them were about to share.

Their hunger grew to new heights, and before she realized what was happening, Shadow felt herself being hoisted into Digger's arms. On reflex, she wrapped her legs around his narrow waist, locking them at the ankles to help keep herself from falling.

He'll never let you fall.

The thought whispered through her head as his strong hands held the backs of her thighs. Digger turned and walked toward the stairs. His mouth never left hers as he carefully carried her toward the second floor, moving with ease as if she weighed nothing at all.

His steps were smooth, and his hold was protective yet gentle. When they got to the top, he headed straight for his room.

Shadow continued feasting on him as if she were starved as he covered the distance between his doorway and the bed. When he got to the edge, Digger lowered her down onto the mattress, settling himself between her thighs.

Her head fell back, and her eyelids closed as she let herself become lost in the moment. There hadn't been many like this in her thirty-two years. Or any, if truth be told.

Not like this. Not like it was with Digger. And they'd only just begun.

Deciding to take more control of the situation, Shadow pushed her palms against his chest. The man above her froze half-a-second before pulling his lips from hers and lifting himself up so he could look her in the eyes.

"What's wrong?" Digger's dark brows bunched together at the center.

But Shadow simply gave him a grin as she shifted her body out from beneath his. Guiding him onto his back, she straddled his terry-clothed hips. Speaking softly, she brought her mouth back down to his.

"Nothing's wrong," she promised. "I just wanted to see more of you. This way makes it so much easier."

Her fingertips traced the curves of his sculpted chest as she began a trail of small, wet kisses along his jaw. The coarse hair of his well-trimmed beard tickled her lips before her mouth moved to the smooth curve of his neck.

A kiss here. A light, playful nibble there. The edge of her teeth bit into him oh so gently, and when they did, Digger's breath hitched, hips thrusting reflexively upward toward hers.

Shadow smiled against the dip of his collar bone as she continued making her way lower. With one hand following the lines of his muscular abs, she put her lips around one of his small, distended nipples.

Digger moaned, the deep sound filling the otherwise silent room as she used her tongue to lick and tease the tiny nub. And when she was finished there, she moved to the other, giving it the same slow, titillating attention as the first.

Shadow wanted to go faster. She wanted to rip off her clothes, pull his towel free, and fill herself with the steel rod that was currently pressing against her throbbing sex. But she forced herself to savor the moment because, as they both knew all too well, tomorrow was never guaranteed.

Moving lower, she slid her body slowly along the length of his. She didn't stop until her feet were hanging halfway off the bed. Rising up onto her knees, she looked down at him with another sensual smile, and then Shadow reached for the towel still knotted around his waist.

The white terrycloth was fully tented, but Digger didn't act embarrassed or ashamed in the least. Given what she'd already felt pressing against the apex of her thighs, she could understand why.

Her fingers dipped between the tanned skin of his lower abs and the thick, white material. She paused just long enough to give him time to change his mind. When he didn't, she pulled the towel free, exposing him in all his glory.

It felt like Christmas morning as she unwrapped the most glorious gift she'd ever been given.

Reaching down, she took him into her hand, curling her fingers as far around his thick rod. Digger hissed in a breath, and she saw his eyes roll shut. Shadow smiled, loving how reactive he was to her touch.

She began sliding her fist up and down his velvet-lined shaft. Using slow, methodical movements, she focused on bringing him as much pleasure as she possible could.

Digger moaned again, his chest rising and falling with increasingly panted breaths. A drop of moisture beaded at the man's swollen tip, and suddenly nothing could keep her from discovering his taste.

Leaning down, Shadow took him fully between her lips. A touch of warm salt hit the tip of her tongue, and she moaned around his length. His body jerked beneath her as she savored that very first taste.

"Damn, princess." His breathy rumble gave away his obvious approval. "That feels so fucking good. But you don't have to—"

"Shhh…" She stopped long enough for a gentle reminder. "I don't *have* to do anything, Dig." Her gaze slid back down to his swollen cock. "Trust me, I *want* to do this."

Not giving him a second's worth of time to further protest, Shadow resumed her previous torture, adding a playful little swirl of her tongue.

Digger reached for her, being careful to steer clear of the bandaged cut. His palm came to a rest at the back of her head. His fist filled with the silky strands of her hair as she moved up and down in slow, salacious slides.

She was cognizant of her recent concussion, but there was only a dull aching of pain remaining. It was nothing compared to the all-consuming pleasure she was giving, and Shadow refused to let it get in her way.

"Oh, yeah," Digger groaned. His breaths becoming even shallower as they came at a more rapid pace.

She licked and sucked to her heart's content, finding the perfect rhythm that seemed to be driving him mad with need. Her head continued bobbing between his strong thighs, bringing him closer and closer to that glorious edge. But just as she was certain the man in her arms was about to explode…

Digger pulled himself free, hauling her up his body and flipping her over, onto her back.

A tiny squeal of surprise escaped Shadow's throat, but then she caught sight of his fiery gaze. His eyes were filled with a burning desire, and she smiled knowing it was all for her.

"My turn," Digger growled.

It was the only warning he gave before the man leaned down, mimicking her every move.

Bringing his mouth to her lips, he kissed her even more thoroughly than before. When he was finished, he moved lower to her jaw, neck, and the dip at the front of her throat.

He rose up, wasting no time divesting her of her black tank-top and bra. With her upper half was bare and lying before him, Digger gave her hardened nipples the same delicious attention she'd given his.

Shadow's back arched high when he took the first peak into his mouth. He was hot. Wet. His talented tongue and lips bringing her closer and closer to Heaven.

When he got his fill there, the incredible man stole another page from her impromptu playbook, using his mouth to follow the shallow line running vertically down the length of her toned abs. Digger reached the waistband of her cotton jogger shorts, and he didn't so much as pause

His fingers dipped between her hips and the tops of her shorts and white lace panties. Shadow lifted her pelvis from the mattress in an effort to help. A ghost of a smirk lifted one corner of the baffling man's lips as he seamlessly pulled the garments over her hips and down the curves of her smooth thighs.

She watched from where she lay fully naked in the center of the bed, taking in her fill of his mouthwatering form. Tanned skin, impressive muscles, and a heart much bigger than the stubborn man realized made him about as perfect of a man as any she'd ever known.

Digger crawled back onto the mattress and brought a hand to her bare sex. Using only his fingers, he began an erotic journey, running a fingertip the length of her slit. Shadow's moan echoed off the white bedroom walls as he doled out the same delectable torture she that had.

His fingers were magic as they played her body like an instrument he'd already mastered. And when he pushed one deep inside her greedy core, she cried out to the heavens above.

In and out, he thrust his hand back and forth between her splayed thighs. She was wet and ready, her body practically begging him for more. And the sweet, selfless man seemed more than happy to oblige.

Leaning down, Digger brought his lips to her swollen, aching clit. And when his tongue flicked the taut bundle of nerves, Shadow cried out, already close to finding the ultimate release.

"Dig!" His shortened nickname flew from her mouth. Her hips pressed higher, her greedy body seeking everything this man was willing to give.

Digger increased his speed and the force of his hand as he continued using his mouth to drive her positively mad. He added a second finger, stretching her body in ways it hadn't been in a long time.

The combination of movements and sensations proved to be damn near lethal. Her legs trembled, and she could feel her impending climax as it climbed higher and higher with every beat of her racing heart.

And just when Shadow was convinced it was possible to die from the erotic pressure, Digger used a little more force with the tip of his tongue, and then…

She began to fly.

* * *

SLADE WAS awestruck as he took in the sight of Shadow lost in the throes of passion. Breathtaking didn't even begin to do the erotic scene justice.

Flushed skin. Disheveled hair. Firm, luscious breasts rising and falling with the sound of her audible breaths.

It was an image he'd already committed to memory.

"Wow." The woman lying naked before him

slowly opened her eyes. Staring up at him through a satiated gaze, she told him lazily, "That was…"

When she appeared to be struggling to find the words, Slade shot her a sideways grin.

"Tell me about it." He let his grin inch closer to an actual smile. "Don't move."

"Don't worry." Shadow didn't hesitate in her response. "I'm pretty sure my legs would just collapse beneath me if I tried."

With a breathy chuckle, Slade turned around and walked unabashedly across the room. He'd noticed earlier that Owens' men had left the go-bag they'd recovered from the cabin on the floor next to the dresser. Squatting down, he unzipped the bag and began to search for the small box he'd tossed into one of the inner pouches at the last minute.

At the time, he and Shadow were planning to be at the cabin for an undetermined number of days, and they had no idea what to expect in the way of threats. And since he'd learned early into his military career that condoms had multiple uses in the field…

Don't be a dumbass. There's only one reason you packed that box, and she's lying on that bed right now waiting for you to return.

He tore open the box and ripped one of the foil squares free before dropping the others back into the gaping bag. With his hands on his knees, he pushed himself back up to his feet. Seconds later, Slade was standing at the edge of the bed.

"I thought maybe you'd changed your mind."

"Not a chance." He tore the small package open, retrieving the protective sheath and rolling it over his aching length.

Shadow smiled, her heavy-lidded eyes following his every move. And when she licked her lips as if she were about to consume a delicious meal, he had to force himself not to pounce.

The mattress dipped beneath him as he rejoined her on the bed. Slade settled himself between her legs, keeping the bulk of his weight balanced with his forearms at either side of her head.

Speaking of her head…

His gaze slid to the injured area on her forehead, the skin around the bandaged cut even darker than it was when they'd first arrived. The same murderous rage he felt toward the person responsible threatened to return.

"I'm okay," she promised him softly. "Really, I am."

She brought a palm to his cheek, the sweet touch creating a rush of emotion he didn't know he possessed. Leaning down, he pressed his mouth to a spot next to the place where she'd been hurt, letting he know without words how sorry he was that she'd been hurt.

"Slade," Shadow whispered his name like a prayer.

He pulled back, feeling as though something

significant had just changed. Not with her, and he hoped like hell nothing ever did. Because as far as he was concerned, she was perfect in every way.

No, the change Slade felt came from a place buried deep within himself. A shifting of sorts, and one he couldn't exactly name. But it was there, and whatever it was he was feeling, it was all because of her.

Her actions. Her amazing heart. And also…her sweet words.

"Say it again."

Shadow frowned, clearly confused by the unexpected command. "Say what? That I really am okay?" she asked softly.

He gave a quick shake of his head. "Not that part," he clarified. "I want to hear you say my name."

A slow and gentle smile lifted both corners of her lips. Her eyes remained locked with his, and with her very next breath, Shadow opened her mouth and whispered his name again.

"Slade."

God, he'd never get tired of hearing that. Not when it was coming from her.

His heart kicked against his ribs, and then it hit him like a ton of bricks. Slade no longer hated the sound of the name.

Before now—before *her*—it had merely served as a constant reminder of the darkness from which he'd been created. When she said it, however…when he heard his name fall from Shadow's lips…Slade realized it was time to leave all that other in the past.

The future, that was what he needed to focus on. It was suddenly the only thing that mattered.

Sure, his past had molded him into the man he was today, and there were some parts he hoped he never forgot. But from this moment on, Slade decided he was going to let the rest of the shit go.

Starting today, he was focusing on being the man Shadow saw when she looked deep into his eyes. Starting now, he made a silent promise to himself to do whatever it took to become the man she deserved.

Because she was what mattered. Shadow, her father, and the rest of the team. They were the family he'd never been given, and thanks to her, he finally understood that was all he'd ever need.

"Make love to me, Slade." She said his name again.

This time, it was accompanied by a request he was more than happy to fulfill.

With his eyes still on hers, Slade reached a hand between their bodies to align himself up to her welcoming core. He hissed a breath when he felt her hot and ready, and as he began pushing his hips forward, he moved gently to avoid causing her pain.

She was tight, and he was larger than average. And since the last thing he ever wanted to do was hurt her, he went slow, giving her body time to adjust to his size.

Shadow's eyes fell shut, and her lips parted with a feathery gasp. At first, he worried he'd hurt her in spite of the care he was taking, but then…she smiled.

"You good?" he asked, because he had to be sure.

Her heated gaze returned to his. "I'm good. You?"

Good? Hell no, I'm not good. I'm fucking fantastic.

"Oh yeah." Slade cleared his throat and nodded. "I'm perfect."

With that all cleared up, he began moving his hips backward and forward in slow, gentle slides. He groaned aloud at the exquisite feel of her core as her inner muscles clenched and worked his body as if she'd been made solely for him.

Home.

The word entered his mind of its own volition, and he couldn't bring himself to fight it. He'd never had a home, not in any real sense of the word. But now…

I never want to leave.

"God, sweetheart," he moaned loudly when her hips rolled upward against his. "You feel so fucking good."

Shadow closed her eyes and let her head fall back, giving herself over to him like an offering he couldn't refuse. And as their bodies worked together in search of the ultimate pleasure, Slade found himself equally excited and terrified, all at the same time.

He was excited because he felt like he'd finally found the one thing he hadn't known he'd been missing. But with that came the unrelenting fear that he'd eventually lose her.

Because that's what life had shown him. Pain. Loss. Disappointment. Those were the lessons life had taught him up to this point. And Slade knew with all he had that if anything ever happened to this woman, every last part of him would be destroyed beyond any hope of repair.

A little fear never hurt anyone.

His former Naval drill sergeant's words floated past his ears. The guy wasn't wrong back then, and he wasn't wrong now.

He wasn't supposed to fall for the boss's daughter. Slade wasn't supposed to fall for anyone at all. But he had, and now…it was too late.

What was happening between him and the woman in his arms far surpassed physical pleasure. It ran deeper. Truer. And truth be told, even if he could, Slade wasn't about to stop it.

"Oh, God, Slade." Shadow panted his name again. "I'm…close."

A wide smile lifted his lips as he thrust a bit harder and picked up the pace. He pushed himself in and out of her molten heat as she rolled her hips against his.

Time stood still as they both became lost in a sea of sensual, sexual joy. And when he angled his hips just so, Slade's name echoed off the wall with Shadow's next cry.

She arched her back high as a low, keening sound

escaped from the back of her throat. He held her close as she came even harder and longer than the time before. Slade grunted and huffed out several harsh breaths as her inner muscles clamped down on him like a vise.

"Ah, fuck." He ground the words out as his own climax grew nearer.

His lower body moved faster and harder, his thrusts becoming uneven in their delivery. As Shadow's muscles began to relax with the final tendrils of her release, Slade's orgasm struck him down with a vengeance.

A deep, guttural, masculine growl flew from his chest as he came. His cock pulsed as he became depleted of his essence, and by the time his climax had passed, he wasn't sure his heart was still beating.

He huffed out a breath before sucking in more much-needed air. Slade repeated the move a half-dozen times before blowing out a breath.

"Holy shit."

"Told ya, it was wow." Shadow teased, her voice slightly strained from being trapped beneath him.

With a below-the-breath curse, Slade pushed himself up to prevent his weight from crushing her completely. Growing serious, he brushed some wayward strands from her face before gently tucking them behind her ear.

"You okay?" he asked, praying he'd done nothing to cause her pain.

She nodded as a genuine smile slowly spread across her face. "Oh yeah. I'm definitely okay."

Slade stole another precious moment, letting himself hold her close without saying a single word. He simply looked at her, taking in the beauty that was Shadow.

And suddenly, for the first time ever, he felt like the luckiest bastard in the world.

CHAPTER 12

The next morning...

Shadow abandoned the computer program that was still working to ID the bomber. She glanced up from where she sat on the couch to glance across the room to where Slade stood.

He was in the kitchen, whipping them up something that smelled absolutely heavenly, and if she wasn't mistaken, the stoic former SEAL was...smiling.

To be fair, she'd been doing a lot of that herself this morning. Smiling. Humming. Remembering.

Memories from the night before—and their unexpected lovemaking session in the shower a couple of hours ago—were still so fresh and all-consuming it was nearly impossible to concentrate on anything else. But she had to.

For her mother and father.

For herself.

Because Michael Stanton was still out there, rubbing elbows with many of the country's top leaders. The asshole was walking around, spending his days as a free man and believing he'd quite literally gotten away with murder.

But Shadow was going to put an end to that even if it was the last thing she ever did. Whatever she had to do, no matter how long it took, she was going to make sure he paid for his crimes.

I won't let him get away with it, Mom. I promise you, I won't.

"Order up!"

Slade's deep voice called to her from the other side of the kitchen's sizeable island. She blinked her thoughts back into the present and refocused on the sexy man staring back at her instead.

Shadow pushed herself to her feet with a smile, secretly wondering when she went to mentally referring to him as Slade, rather than Digger. Her smile grew even more with her very next step, because she knew exactly when the mental change had occurred.

Say it again.

His whispered plea from the night before sounded inside her head. A familiar tingling in her lower belly made its presence known.

Between last night and that morning's mind-blowing scene in the shower, she would have thought her libido would be ready for a break. But as Shadow made her way over to where her sexy personal chef was waiting, she wondered if there would ever be a time when she didn't look at him and crave more.

"This looks amazing, thank you." She walked over to him with the sole purpose of going in for a kiss.

Shadow started to rise onto her tiptoes to reach him, and Slade leaned in to meet her halfway.

"You're welcome." He pressed his lips to hers. "Now go sit down and eat while it's still hot."

"Yes, sir." Shadow gave him her best imitation of a military salute before turning to round the island's end. When she did, he gave her rear a playful slap with his palm. "Hey!" She swung her widened gaze back to him with a mental note to pay him back in full when he least expected it.

Not bothering to hide the breathtaking smile on his rugged face, he motioned to the mounds of food he'd spent the last forty-five minutes preparing.

"Dig in," he handed her a plate and a fork, waiting for her to take her portion first before getting his own.

A gentleman at heart.

After dishing up some of the breakfast casserole he'd so generously made, Shadow slid onto one of the island's four barstools before giving into temptation and taking her first bite.

"Oh, my gosh!" she exclaimed before she'd

finished chewing her food. "This is so good. Where on earth did you learn to cook like this?"

While she took another bite, and then another one after that, Slade dished out a heaping portion of the cheesy egg, onion, and sausage bake he'd created and placed it on his plate.

"I'm self-taught, thank you, very much." He shot her a look. "And you don't have to sound quite so surprised."

"Can't help it." Shadow flashed him a grin as he came around the island to sit on the stool to her left. Using her best British accent, she jutted her chin and tilted her head. "If I've learned anything the last few days, it's that you, sir, are a man of many surprises."

The crooked smile he gave made her heart flip inside her chest.

"Yeah?" Slade flattened his palms against the granite before leaning toward her. "Well, stick around, princess." He gave her a wink. "'Cause you ain't seen nothing yet."

Her shoulders shook with soft laughter as she filled her fork with more of the deliciously savory food. The domesticated moment was interrupted far too soon when her computer released a loud *ding*.

Slade stopped his fork midway to his mouth before turning and looking her way. "What was that?"

"The program got a hit." Shadow shot up from the stool. With hurried steps, she rushed back to the coffee table and spun the device around to see.

"Holy crap!" She sent Slade an excited look from over her shoulder. "It worked!"

"You got him?" he asked, moving toward her like a man on a mission.

Needing to be sure, she turned back and scanned the data that had popped up on the screen. "Andrew Reiner." She began reading what she saw out loud. "Thirty-seven, married, and…" Shadow's breath hitched with a gasp. "No way."

"What?" Slade came to her side, placing a warm hand to the small of her back.

"Look at this." She pointed to the screen and began reading aloud. "This says he's currently employed, and according to last year's tax return, his employer for the past four years is the—"

"Central Intelligence Agency?" His spine grew stiff as a board. "The son of a bitch is CIA?"

"According to the facial rec software, he is."

"And how accurate is the software?"

"Very." But then she admitted, "I'm pretty biased, though, since I am the one who designed it."

"Seriously?"

"Yes, seriously." Shadow's brow arched high. "And you don't have to sound quite so surprised."

With a shake of his head and a roll of his eyes, he brought the conversation back around. "Just want to make sure we don't waste time going after the wrong guy, princess."

"Mmm hmm." Her eyes narrowed with an exaggerated, playful glare. But then she grew serious again as she looked back at the screen, scrolling and scanning for additional information. "No criminal record, top of his class in college, and top half of his class at The Farm." She referred to Camp Peary, which was the CIA's covert training facility near Williamsburg, Virginia. "Finances appear to be in order, he pays his taxes on time, there's no massive debt…" Her fingers tapped against the keys. "And according to his bank statements for the past twelve months, there haven't been any significantly large deposits."

"Could he have a different account you aren't seeing? Like one off-shore?"

"It's possible." Shadow shrugged. "I'll have to do some digging."

"But you're sure he's our guy?"

"I could bore you with all the technical descriptions and steps if you want, or you could just trust me and take me at my word."

His dark eyes lasered in on hers. "I do trust you, Shadow." Slade's throat worked with a hard swallow. "I trust you with my life."

"Then I guess it's time to call in the team, because this"—she pointed to the digital image of Andrew Reiner—"is definitely our guy."

"NOT TO BE THAT GUY, BUT..." Bones turned away from Shadow's computer to look over to where Slade was standing. "Should we maybe turn this information over to the police?"

Slade opened his mouth to explain why they'd decided against that plan, but the woman beside him answered the question before he got the chance.

"It's too risky." Shadow gave her head a definitive shake. "Andrew Reiner's CIA. So was my mom, and though he's clearly done everything in his power to erase any evidence proving it...so was Stanton."

Bones frowned. "You think he has the cops in his pocket?"

"The asshole managed to get a government spook to carry out at least one of the attempted hits on Shadow." Slade shot the other man a serious look. "You tell me."

Falcon nodded. "Digger's right." The sniper's gaze remained on the intel filling the laptop's screen. "For now, we have to assume that anyone in authority has been compromised."

"Authority, hell." Apollo chimed in next. "I say we don't trust anyone outside the team."

Shadow turned a smile in the man's direction. "I always knew you were the smartest one of the bunch. No matter what these guys say about you."

The woman never ceased to amaze him, and Slade couldn't stop the grin curling the corners of his lips. Without thinking, he lifted his hand as if to reach for her. But then he remembered they weren't alone and let it—and his small smile—fall back into place.

He blinked, realizing only then that Bones had been watching him from a few feet away. The nosey medic's eyes twitched with what appeared to be an assessing glance, his gaze dropping to Slade's hand before shifting over to Shadow.

Slade cleared his throat, and the other man blinked. They shared a look, and he knew his friend knew. Or at the very least, Bones had his suspicions.

Well, shit.

Thankfully the other man kept whatever he was thinking from the rest of the room. Instead of embarrassing both Slade and Shadow, Bones picked up where their original conversation left off.

"Okay, so until we hear otherwise, this stays between us."

Apollo looked over at him and asked, "How do we want to proceed?"

"We need to talk to Reiner." Shadow responded before anyone else had the chance.

Slade immediately swung his attention back to her. "There is no *we*, princess." That was a total non-negotiable. "It's just going to be me and the guys."

Fire shot at him from the feisty woman's baby blues. "Like hell. No way you're leaving me out of this. Not when *I'm* the one he's trying to kill."

"That's exactly why I'm not letting you anywhere *near* the son of a bitch."

Shadow blinked, her expression twisting with exaggerated confusion. "Wow. The bonk on the head I got from the explosion must've done a number on my hearing. Because I could have sworn you just said you weren't *letting* me go with you to confront the man who nearly blew both our asses to bits. And, for all we know also shot up the motel."

"You heard right."

"Dammit Slade, I'm going with you."

But Slade simply put his hands on his hips and leaned in, lowering his voice when he told her with clear enunciation, "No, you're not."

"Yes." She seethed. "I *am.*"

"Uh…kids?" Bones stepped toward them, his wary gaze bouncing between them. "Is everything okay here?"

"Everything's fine," Slade grumbled sharply. "She's just apparently forgotten that she's not the one calling the shots."

"*She* is right here and can speak for herself. And I refuse to be left alone in this apartment while you guys go off to fight *my* battles for me!"

"Never said you'd be staying here alone."

"Well, if you and the guys are going after Reiner, then who—"

The door to the apartment opened and, right on cue, Rafe Owens stepped inside.

"You've got to be kidding me." Shadow stared at the man who'd just crossed the threshold before turning her fiery gaze back on Slade. "You seriously called my dad?"

"You seem to forget that your dad is also our boss," he reminded her. "And I didn't call. I texted."

"Semantics." She fumed.

"Relax, darling." Owens joined them. "I'm just here to keep you company while they have a talk with our suspect."

"Andrew Reiner's more than a suspect. My program positively identified him as the bomber, and I want to be there when he's—"

"I'm afraid this isn't about what you want." Owens interrupted her. "It's about keeping you safe. Which, in case there was any question regarding the matter, is our number one goal."

Her blonde hair swayed back and forth with a shake of her head. "Our only goal should be bringing Michael Stanton to his knees."

"And we will," Slade vowed. "But not at your expense."

"That's not your call."

"No, but it *is* mine," Shadow's father reminded her. A beat later, the powerful man turned his intense stare Slade's way. "Go." He used his salt-and-peppered chin to motion for the door. "I've got her."

With a dip of his head, Slade acknowledged his boss's order before sliding a quick glance Shadow's way. The woman looked made enough to spit nails.

He wanted nothing more than to pull her into his

arms and hold her close until she could finally understand his true motive in leaving her behind. She was so hellbent on being the one to take down her attackers she couldn't see that he was doing everything in his power to keep her safe. And since she clearly wasn't ready to listen to reason…

Keeping his gaze locked onto hers for a full two seconds longer, he said nothing before turning and walking away.

"So." Bones spoke in a hushed tone as he hung back to walk with Slade as the team headed from the apartment to the elevator down the hall. "You and Shadow, huh?"

Slade's chest tightened as he worked like hell to school his expression. "Me and Shadow what?"

"Oh, so that's what we're doing?" The other man sighed. "Come on, man. I saw the way you two were going at each other in there. We all did."

"What you saw was a woman who's pissed because she can't tag along while the trained operatives go after the guy who almost killed us."

"True." Bones didn't so much as attempt to deny the claim. "I also heard you call her 'princess'."

Slade's brows dipped together with a frown. He thought back to the heated exchange but couldn't recall every word that was spoken.

"She hates it when I call her that."

"Oh, so you were just poking the bear, is that it?"

"Pretty much."

He could *feel* the other man's disbelieving stare but continued on down the hall as if the conversation had come to an end. Of course, Bones being Bones, the infuriating medic couldn't keep himself from pushing for more.

"Really? Because the tension between you two sure seemed like there was a lot more going on. Like maybe you've been poking more than the—"

"Finish that sentence, and Andrew Reiner won't be the only one getting his ass kicked today." Slade sent his teammate a warning stare, his tone as lethal as he'd ever used.

He loved Bones like a brother to the point he wouldn't think twice about laying down his life for the other man's. But this was Shadow, and he wasn't about to allow anyone get away with disrespecting her in any sort of way.

Not even another member of his own team.

To his credit, Bones didn't flinch or try to defend his insinuating comment in any way. Instead, the dumbass met Slade's gaze and then…he smiled.

"I'll be damned." The other man gave an approving nod. "Never thought I'd live to see the day. I'll admit this was not one I saw coming, but I also can't say I'm all that surprised."

"What the hell are you rambling on about?"

"Oh, nothin' much. Just the fact that you're head over boots for our girl."

"Our girl?"

She wasn't theirs. Shadow belonged to *him.* He was just too chickenshit to admit it to the guys.

"Don't think I didn't catch the way you started to reach for her earlier." Bones grinned. "Between that, the way you two were shooting daggers at each other, the adorable nickname you gave her, and how defensive you're acting…" Bones shook his head and chuckled. "I mean, you can deny it all you want, brother, but I know a man in love when I see him."

In love?

"I'm not—"

"It's okay, Dig. Really." Bones slapped a hand on Slade's shoulder, giving the muscles there a friendly, supportive squeeze. "In fact, I think I speak for the rest of the team when I say…it's about damn time."

Slade opened his mouth, ready to finish the point he'd been trying to make. But something strong and determined reached up from his heart and stopped him before he could lie.

Holy shit. I love her.

The realization nearly caused him to lose his footing right there in the hall. Sure his feelings for the maddening beauty were growing stronger, but love? He'd never been in love with a woman in his entire life.

Just because it's never happened before doesn't mean it never will.

The four-man team got onto the elevator and began their descent from the fifth floor to the first.

Slade didn't speak the entire ride down to the lobby. He refrained from uttering a single word as they walked half-a-block to where the team's SUV was parked.

As he and the others began the ten-minute drive to Andrew Reiner's home, Slade's mind became filled with thoughts of Shadow and what Bones had said.

She needs to know how you really feel.

Fear raced through his veins at the thought of putting himself into such a vulnerable position. Then again, Slade had never been one to let fear stop him from doing the right thing.

I'll tell her the truth the first chance I get. Just as soon as I get done beating Andrew Reiner's ass.

CHAPTER 13

SHADOW STOOD ON THE BALCONY, ARMS CROSSED AND hair blowing in the breeze. She looked out over the city below.

Buildings, short and tall. Construction crews and cranes. Cars driving this way and that, their owners oblivious to the trail of violence a United States senator had brought to their city.

Oh, the exploding SUV had made the news. Of that, she was certain. But thanks to her father's influence and political connections—as well as her expert computer hacking skills—her face and name, the team's, and her father's company would not be mentioned on TV, social media, or anywhere else.

Rafe Owens is nothing if not thorough.

Shadow sighed, her mind recounting all she'd done to help with the cause.

For starters, once she'd downloaded the hospital

security footage to use for her facial rec software, she'd uploaded an irreversible virus into the files to prevent anyone else from gaining access after the fact. After that, it was a matter of giving the program time to do its thing until they got a positive ID on Reiner.

She sucked in a breath as memories of how she'd spent that time rolled over her in waves. Sex with Slade had been…she didn't even have the words for what it was.

Amazing. Incredible. Mind-blowing. Unforgettable.

In bed. The shower. Both times had been all those things and more. Shadow had a feeling it didn't matter how many times she slept with the former SEAL. The truth was, she'd never get her fill.

But then he'd left her behind, cutting her out of the most important fight of her life. And she was stuck here, being babysat by her father with nothing to do but wait.

"You do know he's only trying to protect you."

Shadow looked to her left as her father came to a stop at her side. His gaze scanned the city below.

"I should be with them."

"You are exactly where you need to be."

"Bullshit." She turned to fully face him. "I need to be out there, Dad. I wanted to be the one looking into Andrew Reiner's beady eyes when he admits Stanton hired him to kill me. I've earned that much, don't you think?"

"It's not about what you've earned, sweetheart."

Her father brought his intelligent stare to hers. "It's about making sure those bastards don't get another chance to hurt you."

"Are you saying you don't trust the team's abilities to keep me safe?"

Emotion filled the powerful man's gaze. "I trust those four men with my life and yours. But you're not just Tac Ops' overwatch. You're my daughter. My flesh and blood. And you're the only family I have left. So no." He gave a shake of his head. "When it comes to you and your safety, I'm not sure I trust anyone completely."

"Not even Slade?" she challenged, knowing full well he wouldn't have locked her away in a cabin in the wood with the man if he didn't trust him.

"Mr. Garrison is the team leader," her father countered. "It only makes sense that he would be the one I'd ask to serve as your bodyguard."

That was such a cop-out answer, and the man damn well knew it.

Knowing the debate was going nowhere, Shadow turned and walked back inside the apartment. Okay, so she may have stormed a bit, but dammit, she was *mad*.

This whole thing started because of the time and effort she'd put into trying to link Stanton to her mother's death. While it may have admittedly gone off the rails far sooner than she'd expected—mainly because Stanton had clearly recognized her without her having realized it when she'd been stalking him in Ohio—but still.

She was my mom. I'm the one who watched her die. I'm the one who sat in that house, crying and terrified that the man who'd done it would come back and kill me, too.

The bastard may have let her live that night, but Shadow knew to her soul that he was the one behind the recent attempts on her life. And the only reason he'd want her dead now was if he was afraid of the world learning the truth about who and what he really was.

And that meant she couldn't give up. Not now. Not until he was either rotting in prison or buried six feet under.

I'll take six feet under for a thousand, please.

"I understand your frustration with having to stay behind." Her father joined her in the kitchen. "Trust me, I'd enjoy a few minutes with that bastard Reiner, myself."

"It's your team, remember?" Shadow opened the fridge and pulled out a bottle of water. "You're the boss. You can do whatever you want."

"You're right. I am, and I can." There was a slight bite in her father's tone. "And what I wanted more than revenge was to be here, with you. To see you with my own eyes, and to know that you were safe."

Shadow's watery gaze lifted to his from the across

the island. "He killed her, Dad. Stanton killed Mom, and now he's tried to kill me."

"I know."

"We have to stop him."

"And we will. But what I can't do…" His voice thickened before he gave a quick clearing of his throat. "What I *won't* do is let my anger and grief for what happened to your mother all those years ago put you in harm's way."

The man who'd raised her the very best way he knew how rounded the island's edge. Her father came to a stop inches from where she stood.

"Your mother was my whole world, Alice." He used her given name. "And then she gave me you, and that world was forever changed. I was devastated when I got the call that your mother was gone." Unshed tears filled the man's sincere gaze. "My heart felt as though it had been ripped right out of my chest. She was my soul mate. My other half." Her father swallowed hard. "I didn't know how to live the rest of my life without her. Part of me didn't want to even try. But I had to go on because I had you. And you needed me then, more than ever before."

"Dad…"

"Raising you has been my greatest accomplishment, sweet girl. I may have made a lot of mistakes along the way, but you are the very best part of me. So you can be upset at me if you want, but if anything were to ever happen to you…" His typically strong voice cracked. "That's the one thing I don't think I'd be able to survive."

Well, crap.

Shadow took a step forward, feeling like the most ungrateful daughter on the face of the planet. Suddenly wanting nothing more than to wrap her arms around the best dad a girl could ever have, she took a step forward and lifted her arms. But just as she moved, the apartment's landline phone began to ring, taking both her and her father off guard.

"Do you think it's them?" she asked, referring to the team.

But her father shook his head as he walked out of the kitchen to the living room end table where the phone sat waiting. "They'd call my cell." He reached down and tapped a button, putting the call on speaker so they both could hear. "Yes?"

"Mr. Cavanagh?" A young man's voice came through the speaker.

"This is he."

Shadow immediately recognized the alias as one her father had used during his days with MI6. Apparently, he'd also used it when signing the apartment's lease so the space would be safe from anyone trying to find the person or persons hiding out under the team's protection.

It's me. That person is me.

"Mr. Cavanagh, this is Darren from building security. I just wanted to let you know the fire department sent over a couple of guys to check out that gas leak you reported. They're on their way up to your apartment now."

"Gas leak?" Shadow didn't bother keeping her voice low.

Her father frowned as he let the other man know, "I'm afraid there's been some mistake. No one here reported a gas leak."

A slight pause ensued as Darren presumably processed the information he'd just been given. "Really?" The young man sounded genuinely surprised. "That's weird because those guys seemed quite sure that *you* were the one who called nine-one-one."

"Well, they were wrong. Like I said, no one here called anyone about a—"

The door to the apartment didn't just bust open then. The entire thing was blown right off its damn hinges.

What followed took less than a handful of minutes to transpire.

Shadow screamed in surprise, her hair whipping around her head as her eyes flew to where the door used to stand tall. A black cannister she recognized instantly was thrown deep inside the apartment.

The flash bang rolled, smoke billowing up from its top as her father yelled out for her to take cover.

"Get down!" His deep voice bellowed as he bolted in her direction.

A second later, the device detonated with a blinding flash of light and a deafening *bang*.

Shadow turned away on reflex as her father did the same. She looked back in time to see a man dressed all in black sucker punch her father in the face.

"Dad!"

Feeling disoriented, she tried going to him, but a set of meaty arms wrapped around her from behind.

No!

The sound of glass shattering and fists hitting flesh traveled through the ringing still present in her ears. Panic didn't just settle in, it took over in an instant. But then Shadow remembered her training. While it was true, she wasn't as strong or skilled as Slade and the others, her father had made sure she at least knew some basic self-defense moves.

She stomped a sneakered heel as hard as she could down onto one set of her attacker's booted toes. Thankfully, they weren't protected with steel, and the guy behind her cried out in pain.

His hold on her loosened, and she took full advantage, bringing both of her arms up in one quick move. The strategy worked, lifting the man's arms enough to give her room to slip her body free from his grasp. Shadow spun around, kicked the man in the gut, inwardly smiling when he lost his footing and fell back on his ass.

She turned to see her father engaged in a serious

battle of hand-to-hand combat. A gun went flying out of his assailant's hand, sliding across the tiled floor not far from where she stood.

Having stupidly left her own pistol on the nightstand upstairs, Shadow raced for the deadly weapon that had come to a rest a few feet away.

She bent down, her fingers touching the gun's cool metal. But just as she started to curl her fingers around it, the same boot she'd stomped on kicked the pistol free from her hand.

"Ah!" Shadow cried out when she felt the cracking of bone.

Pain exploded as her pinky finger was forced into an unnatural angle. The nauseating burn radiated up into her hand and wrist, and beyond.

Son of a—

The man in black swung his foot toward her midsection next, his boot slamming into her stomach and ribs with such force, she flew over and onto her back.

"Alice!" her father called out her name.

She coughed and gasped, fire igniting in her ribs as her lungs tried and failed to find air. Shadow tried her best to ignore the pain. To roll over onto her side and push herself up to her feet.

But just as she thought she might actually succeed, that same boot landed a vicious blow to the side of her head.

She fell back, her already injured head bouncing

off the room's unforgiving tile. Her mouth became filled with the metallic taste of blood.

With a barely conscious groan, Shadow turned her head and spit out as much of her own blood as she could. It was only then that she realized she hadn't heard her father say anything more.

Her blurred gaze looked over to where he lay on the floor. His eyes were closed, and he was no longer moving.

At first, she feared the worst had happened, and he was dead. But then she saw the man next to him stand up with an empty syringe grasped tightly in his hand.

Oh, God!

Shadow felt a sharp sting, and she immediately knew what had happened. The asshole she'd been fighting had just injected her with the same drug they'd given her dad.

Whatever it was, it worked impressively fast, and within seconds, the world around her began to fade. The last thing Shadow saw was her father's still, unmoving face. The last thing she felt was regret.

I'm…sorry…Slade.

The thought whispered its way through her muddled mind half a second before the drugs fully took effect. When they did, any pain and fear she'd felt earlier vanished…just like everything else.

* * *

SLADE SAT in the parked SUV, watching the house across the street. Andrew Reiner and his wife lived in one of Charlotte's upscale neighborhoods. It wasn't gated, but even if it were, he wouldn't have cared.

Thanks to a quick social media search Falcon had done on the drive over, they'd quickly confirmed Reiner's wife wasn't at home, but rather out of the country for work. According to her latest post, made only a few hours prior to their arrival, Mrs. Reiner—who worked for a major marketing firm—was in Hong Kong until next week.

It still amazed him how freely people volunteered such information. Especially on platforms so easily accessible and easy to hack. In this case, however, the information proved quite useful.

With her out of the way, and since the couple had no children, the chances of an innocent getting in the crossfire were slim to non-existent.

"You sure you don't want me to call Shadow?" Apollo asked from the passenger seat. "We could have her hack into Reiner's security system, so he isn't alerted when we go inside."

"I'm not worried about him calling the cops." Slade kept his eyes on the two-story brick colonial home. "What's he going to say? That four of the five people he almost killed with a bomb he set have broken into his house?"

"The man does have a point," Bones chimed.

Slade met the medic's gaze from the rearview mirror and gave him a nod.

"Okay, boys." Falcon spoke up next. "We ready to do this, or what?"

To go face-to-face with the man who tried to take Shadow away from him forever? Oh, yeah. He was more than fucking ready.

"Still going with the shock and awe approach, Dig?" Apollo looked at him for the answer.

Slade nodded in the affirmative before opening his door. It was broad daylight, and there was a good chance any number of their neighbors were watching from their windows.

He didn't care.

When they got to the home's quaint front stoop, Slade pulled the small breaching device he'd picked up from the office before making their way here. The low-NEQ assault IED disrupter. Compact and lightweight, the device fit in the palm of his hand.

As a SEAL, and then later as Tac-Ops' demolitions expert, he'd used ones just like it in the field dozens of times. Working quickly, he placed the device on the interior portion of the doorjamb, next to the gold-colored deadbolt.

He stepped to the side and made sure his team was out of the way. And then…

The device was ignited, and the door burst open with a small blast. Pulling their pistols from their waistbands, Slade and the others entered the home as if they were S.W.A.T. going in for a raid.

Room-by-room, the four operatives efficiently cleared the house with Bones and Falcon taking the second floor. Slade went left, checking the home's formal living room and den while Apollo went right.

After his teammate cleared the dining room and kitchen, they regrouped near the home's expansive mudroom and half-bath.

"Upstairs is clear," Apollo announced as he and Bones made their way back down the stairs. "No sign of Reiner or evidence connecting him to the bomb."

"It's here." Slade looked back at his teammate. "We just have to keep looking."

"Uh, no offense, Dig…" Bones shot him an uncertain stare. "But this guy could've hired someone else to build the bomb for him. Or hell, he could've done his planning and constructing at a different location that couldn't be traced back to him."

"I don't think so." He shook his head, slowly walking back through the den. As he scanned the room for anything out of place, his gut was screaming at him that the evidence was here. "From what I read in Shadow's intel on the guy, Reiner's a mid-level agent who's only been with the agency a couple of years. The bulk of their money seems to come from his wife's corporate job."

"So?"

"So, on paper, at least, this guy doesn't feel like he's been on the wrong side of things for very long."

It was total conjecture, and Slade wasn't even sure why his gut was leading him down that path. But the lack of strange activity in the guy's finances made him think Reiner wasn't necessarily a willing participant in Stanton's game.

"Hey, what's this?" Falcon ran a gloved hand over the edge of one of the room's wooden bookshelves. "This board is different from the other shelves. And it feels loose. Almost like you could..."

They watched as their teammate pushed the board in with the palm of his hand. A soft clicking sound reached Slade's, and a beat later, the shelf began to move.

The hell?

"Holy shit!" Bones exclaimed. "The guy's got a secret room!"

Thinking perhaps he'd underestimated their current target, Slade went to the hidden entrance. A light flickered to life as he led his team into the shadowed space. And when he saw the pictures taped to the small room's back wall, he instantly felt sick.

Shadow.

There were at least a dozen pictures. And she was in every single one.

"Son of a bitch." Falcon studied them closely.

Apollo and Bones both grumbled their own string of curses beneath their breaths.

Slade understood why they were enraged by the disturbing sight. Shadow was a member of Tac-Ops, and now they knew beyond a shadow of a doubt that she'd been specifically targeted. So of course, these guys wanted to rip the man responsible to shreds.

But no matter how infuriated his teammates were, their rage toward Reiner didn't hold a candle to Slade's. Because they weren't in love with Shadow. They hadn't spent last night in her arms.

Slade did, and he had. And seeing the printed images of her…and even some that were zoomed out enough to also include him… That didn't make him simply want to kill the slimy bastard.

I want to torture him slowly and without so much as an ounce of fucking mercy.

"Uh…Dig?" Apollo's wary tone pulled Slade from his murderous thoughts. "We have a problem." The man looked over at him before pointing to a specific image on the wall. "A big one."

Slade walked back over to where Apollo was standing. He passed by a small table holding remnants of the same kind of explosive that had been used on his car. He looked at the picture Apollo's index finger was still on, his heart sinking when he realized what had the other man so concerned.

The apartment.

The bastard had taken a picture of the apartment building where he and Shadow had stayed the night before. The same place where she and her father were now. And he'd left her there, thinking she was safe.

Son of a…

"The apartment's been compromised," he announced to the team. "We have to get back there. *Now!*"

Slade spun on his heels and made a beeline for the room's hidden entrance. As he and the others rushed from the house, he pulled out his phone and called Shadow's new number.

It rang and rang, but nobody answered. He tried again with the same disheartening results.

"Rafe's not picking up," Bones announced after two failed attempts to reach their boss.

Apollo added to the terrifying news by sharing, "No one's answering the apartment's landline, either."

She's okay. They have to be okay.

Slade couldn't allow himself to think anything else. But as he and his teammates sprinted across the street to their SUV, he couldn't help but acknowledge the ball of dread and fear growing deep in his gut.

The thought of something happening to Rafe was enough to bring him to his knees. But the thought of losing Shadow forever…

I can't lose her now. Not like this. Not fucking ever.

And as he drove like a bat out of hell back to where he'd left her and her father, the same thought played on a loop over and over again in his head.

She's okay.

She's okay.

She's okay.

Slade's grip on the steering wheel became white-knuckled because if he was wrong…if the worst had happened, and Rafe and the woman he loved had been killed…even God wouldn't be able to help the ones responsible for their deaths.

She's okay.

She's okay.

She has to be okay.

CHAPTER 14

"ALICE."

Shadow woke to her father's voice, the sound of her name cutting through the dense and heavy fog. It was low and hushed, almost hollow as it reached her ears, and though she couldn't be sure, the unshakable man sounded as though he were afraid.

"Alice."

She heard her name again as she fought against the pain. Her head pounded and ached to the point she thought it might actually split in two. The left side of her face throbbed to the beat of her heart, and the taste of blood was still present on the tip of her tongue.

"Shadow!"

Her father's call came a bit louder as he switched to using the name she identified with most of all. Sensing the urgency in the man's otherwise stoic and calm demeanor, Shadow forced her eyelids to open despite the harsh lighting shining down on them from up above.

"Dad?" she croaked, her throat and mouth desert dry from whatever drugs the assholes had used. "Where are w—"

Shadow gasped before she could finish asking where they'd been taken, her lungs freezing mid-pull from the sudden and sharp pain in her right side. And…holy *shit*, did it hurt to breathe.

"Oh, thank God." Her father's relief was more than obvious.

Shadow looked around, taking in the small room where they were being held. Her blurred vision cleared a little more as she blinked, and soon their horrifying reality fully set in.

She and her father were each in their own chairs, positioned side-by-side in the middle of a small, and otherwise empty, room. Their hands had been duct taped to the arms of their chairs, and they were surrounded by nothing but bare, concrete walls.

"I don't…understand." She grunted between words, doing her best to ignore the fire burning beneath her ribs as she pulled and tugged in an effort to get her wrists free. "Not that I'm…complaining, mind you, but…why aren't we…dead?"

Their situation was less than ideal, and they were most definitely on borrowed time. But at least they were both still breathing.

"I don't know." Her father shook his graying head. His left eye was bruised and slightly swollen, and a trickle of blood had dried against his bearded chin at one corner of his mouth.

The sight pissed her off as much as it broke her heart. No one got away with hurting her dad.

Not much you can do about it with your hands taped to a freaking chair.

A thought struck, and Shadow's movements froze. Because she may not know how to get out of a situation such as this, but her father had spent years as an operative for MI6.

"Wait, didn't they train you on how to escape situations like this back in the day?"

"They did." He dipped his head in a nod.

"Then why haven't you—"

"I've been waiting."

Waiting? "For what, an invitation?"

Her father didn't respond with anything more than a smile.

Shadow opened her mouth to ask if perhaps the thugs who'd broken into the apartment caused some sort of internal brain bleed. But then she saw the gleaming in his eyes, and she knew.

"You have a plan." Her heart thumped, sending a hefty dose of hope flourishing throughout her system.

"Yes, but I needed you to be awake for it to work."

"What if they'd come back to kill us before I came to?"

"If they wanted us dead, they would have killed us in the apartment."

The apartment.

"How did they even find us?"

"I have no idea. They must have followed you and Digger from the office."

"That's impossible." Shadow started to shake her head but was stopped with a wince as pain shot like a knife through her skull. "Slade made sure we didn't have a tail."

"Well right now, the how doesn't matter. Whoever it is will be coming back, most likely sooner, rather than later. And when they do, we need to be ready."

"Tell me what I need to do."

"We must maintain the element of surprise, which means we have to remain bound until the very last second. And you have to wait for me to make the call."

"Done." She didn't so much as hesitate to agree. "Now hurry up and tell me the plan before the assholes come back."

Over the next few minutes, her father did just that. And when the door to the room opened, Shadow was convinced she was ready.

But then she saw the face of the man who'd just entered the room, and just like that, she forgot all about the well-thought-out plan.

"You."

Michael Stanton appeared in his typical black suit

and matching tie. There was even a small pin of the American Flag attached to his lapel.

The sight of the man made her sick, and she began pulling against the tape holding her in place. "You son of a bitch! I swear to God, when I get loose, I'm going to fucking *kill* you!"

Her shouted warning echoed off the concrete walls, but Stanton simply threw his head back and laughed. The bastard *laughed*, and when Shadow looked over at her father, his only response was a slow shake of his head.

Not yet.

She could practically hear his thoughts as his eyes burned into hers with an insistent stare. He'd warned her the waiting would be the hardest part, but until now, she had no idea how true that really was.

"You have your mother's spirit, I'll give you that." Stanton grinned. "And it appears you also inherited both her and your father's do-gooder genes. I warned her, you know. Said those good intentions of hers would end up getting her killed. But like you…" He pulled a pistol from his jacket pocket and sighed. "She refused to listen."

"What did she have on you?" her father asked the man who'd brutally his wife. "I mean, you're going to kill us anyway, the least you could do is give us that."

Stanton looked at her father and then to her before giving one of his shoulders a shrug. "You're right. I am going to kill you."

"Then what are you waiting for, Stanton?" Shadow popped off to the murdering SOB. "Why all the grandstanding? Are you really that hard-up? Let me guess. The missus just doesn't do it for ya, anymore, is that it?"

The man chuckled again. "Damn, Alice. You really are the spitting image of your mother, aren't you?"

"That's the nicest thing a piece of shit like you could ever say. But hey, since you have such a captive audience, why not give us the goods before ending all the fun?" She made a show of her secured hands and shrugged. "Not like we're going anywhere."

He stared down at her with a look of both fury and intrigue. "All right, fine." Stanton began pacing the space between them and the room's only exit. "I suppose I have a few moments to spare before I have to leave for my next speaking event. So yeah, I'll play. Why not?"

Why not, indeed?

Shadow forced her split lip into a smile, the move splitting apart a cut in her lip from earlier. A fresh drop of warm blood began to run down her chin, but she ignored it and focused on every word the murdering asshole spoke.

"I'm assuming you already know that your mother and I were wet work agents with the CIA back in the day," Stanton began. "We were one of the few sets of partners who regularly worked together to take out high-value targets. Oh, they were all very bad people, of course. Your mother never would have done that kind of work otherwise. Amanda was truly a patriot. The woman was just and fair and had one of the biggest hearts I'd ever seen."

"And yet, you had no qualms about putting a bullet into the back of her head while she slept." Shadow glared. "So what kind of person does that make you?"

His blue eyes turned her way, and he momentarily halted his steps. "From where I'm currently standing?" Stanton arched a cocky brow. "I'd say I'm the kind of person who wins."

"No matter the cost, right?" Her father somehow managed to keep his cool.

Given that Stanton had shot and killed the woman her father had called his soulmate, Shadow wasn't sure how her father could remain so calm.

If someone killed Slade, she'd go all scorched earth on their ass. And they'd only shared one magical night together, followed by one glorious morning.

And then I yelled at him right before he left, and all he'd been doing was trying to protect me.

Guilt assaulted her in waves, but she pushed it back. With the silent vow to do whatever was needed to make things right between her and the man she loved, Shadow stared up at the man who'd destroyed her family when she was only six years old.

"So what was it?" She demanded to know. "Did

my mom catch you stealing money from one of the men you two took out?"

Stanton's cold smile gave her chills.

"I'm a lot of things, dear Alice. But I am no thief. What your mother had the unfortunate luck to discover wasn't what I stole, but rather what I'd sold."

"Intel," her father guessed from the chair beside her. "You were a double agent."

"Do you have any idea how much money our country's enemies are willing to pay for classified information? I'll give you a hint." Stanton paused dramatically before lowering his voice to a hushed, "It's a lot."

"So you killed my mom because she found out you were a traitor?"

"Amanda left me no choice!" He lost his cool composure. "The bitch gave me an ultimatum. Either I turn in my notice and cut all ties with my buyers or she was going to turn me in."

"Call my wife a bitch again, Stanton, and see what happens."

The other man simply laughed. "Oh, Rafe. I have missed you, my friend."

"I'm not your fucking friend."

"So you sold government secrets, and Mom threatened to expose you. That's it?"

"That's not enough?" His blue glare swung her way. Stepping toward her, he stopped inches from where she sat. "My life would have been over, Alice.

You were too young to understand that, but I'm sure you can see now that I did what I had to do."

"The only thing I see is a pathetic man who couldn't make it on his own, so he had to cheat his way to the top. Bet your wife and son have no idea, do they? Wonder what your kid would say if he found out his dad was nothing but a greedy, lying, traitorous murdering son of a—"

Stanton's hand flew toward her with such speed, Shadow didn't have time to even try to brace herself for the blow. Pain erupted across the right side of her jaw when the back of his hand struck hard, sending a flash of tiny, white dots twinkling before her watering eyes.

"You bastard!" Her father finally showed some real anger toward their captor. "Touch her again, and I swear to God, I will—"

"What?" Stanton turned his way, pulling a pistol from his suit pocket and keeping it at his side. "What exactly are you going to do to me, Rafe? You going to shoot me? Oh, wait. You can't. In fact, you can't do much of anything can you? Not for your daughter now. And not for your bitch of a wife back then."

Forcing her way through the pain, Shadow looked to where her father remained seated. Her chest tightened with the pain she found swimming in his grief-stricken eyes, but her fists curled when his expression soon turned into stone.

Her father stared the other man down, looking

about as lethal as she'd ever seen him. A beat later, he slid his calculated gaze in her direction. And then he uttered one simple word.

"Now."

It was the only thing he needed to say. The very cue she'd been waiting for her father to give. And now that he had, Shadow began the planned countdown in her head.

Three…two…

Both she and her father went straight into action in a simultaneous move to break themselves free. Just as he'd explained before Stanton came into the room, Shadow gave both her arms a hard jerk as if to bring her fist straight up to her chest.

Despite her father's reassurance, she was still taken by surprise when the duct tape ripped with efficient ease. Shadow jumped to her feet, more than ready to finally take on the man she'd been hunting, but her father had literally beat her to the punch.

Shocked by their unexpected escape from the bindings his men had presumably constructed, Stanton wasn't ready for the meaty fist that had just slammed into his jaw. His head flew to the side, and he stumbled back a few steps from the force. He didn't go all the way down, however, and recovered quickly from her father's hard punch.

As the jerk started to raise his weapon, Shadow spun around and grabbed her chair. It was solid wood and heavy as hell, but she ignored the pain in her battered body and swung it toward him as hard as she could.

Stanton cried out as the chair's legs struck him across the back. A shot rang out, the bullet going wild and slamming into the concrete wall to her left.

"Fucking bitch!"

He started to swing the barrel toward her with the clear intention of shooting her dead. Before he got the chance, her father grabbed for the gun.

The two men immediately became enthralled in a fight to the death. Shadow stood to the side, desperate to find a way to help. But her father and Stanton were both struggling to regain control of the weapon, and if she got in the middle, she might make matters worse.

Their bodies twisted this way and that as their hands and arms became intertwined. And when the gun blasted again, she thought for sure it was finally over.

Then the unthinkable happened, and her father stumbled back. He looked down at the place where Stanton's bullet had struck.

No!

Shadow charged at Stanton, releasing an animalistic growl. She didn't feel the pain in her ribs or the pounding in her head. She only felt a rage unlike any she'd ever known.

Her body slammed into his, and they both tumbled to the floor. The gun in Stanton's hand went flying, sliding across the concrete past her injured father. Without missing a beat, Shadow turned and punched Stanton square in the jaw.

Once.

Twice.

On the third strike, she heard the crunching of bone.

And then, just because it felt too damn good not to, Shadow grabbed two fists of the man's silver hair, and she slammed his head against the unforgiving wall.

His eyes rolled in the back of his head half a second before his entire body grew limp. With him incapacitated for the time being, she pushed herself up and ran to where her father still stood.

"Dad!" Her hands went to his wound as his strong legs gave out beneath him.

Thick, crimson blood oozed from the through her fingers. Her hands became covered with the stuff as tears fell freely from her eyes.

Behind her, Shadow sensed before she saw Stanton stirring back to life. She looked over to where the gun had come to a rest, but a quick calculation in her head said she'd never make it there in time.

"It's okay, sweet girl." Her father brought a trembling hand to the side of her face. His pain-riddled gaze held a moment of clarity long enough for him to tell her quietly, "You know…what …to do."

His eyes lowered as if he were looking down,

toward his belt. He was telling her without words to continue on with the plan.

But their original plan had been destroyed the second that bastard pulled his trigger. Her father wasn't supposed to get shot. This wasn't how *any* of this was supposed to go down.

Plans change, princess. You can either adapt to those changes or die.

The words were her father's from earlier, when he'd been explaining the plan, and she'd started in with the what-ifs. But in her head, it wasn't his voice she was hearing. Instead, it was…

Slade's.

If he were here, he'd be telling her the same thing, of that she was certain. And since he wasn't here and her father was in no position to fight, it was up to her to finish what had been started.

Twenty-six years ago, Michael Stanton made a choice that led them here, to this very moment. He'd started this war long before she understood what that even meant.

He may have started it, but I'm damn well going to end it. Starting now.

Making a show of putting pressure on the wound in her father's lower belly, Shadow hunched herself more so Stanton wouldn't see the move she was making with her right hand.

She found the tiny button hidden behind the buckle of her father's belt. The one he'd told her about shortly before the man who'd shot him entered the room.

Giving it a push, the button released the small blade that had been hidden within the belt's thick leather strap. She palmed the weapon in her balled-up fist, but she didn't make her move right away.

Instead, Shadow leaned up and pressed her lips to her father's forehead. Tears fell from her eyes onto his paling skin below, and it took everything in her not to howl out in anguish.

"I love you, Dad," she whispered softy.

Their eyes met, and she knew he knew. Her father loved her, too. There had never been a day she'd ever doubted that fact. And just as he'd spent his life protecting her, Shadow knew it was time to risk hers in order to save them both.

Shadow pushed herself to her feet, the small knife still concealed in her bloodied fist. She turned and faced the man who wanted her dead and then…

She smiled.

CHAPTER 15

Slade stood in the apartment's entrance, his heart feeling as though it were slowly being ripped in two. The place was trashed with clear signs of one hell of a struggle. Toppled lamps, shattered glass, and splatters of blood marring the formerly pristine space.

I left her here.

His gut churned with nausea as he battled against the rush of bile racing toward his throat. Not only had he left her there, but he'd also ordered her to stay.

And now…

She and Rafe are gone.

His boss and the man's daughter. A woman Slade had fallen in love with in the blink of an eye. But even as he thought it, he knew that wasn't true. Part of him had loved her ever since the team's very first mission. He'd fallen in love with a voice that had been filled with equal amounts of sugar and sass.

Shadow was always there, doing everything she could to keep him and the rest of his team safe. She worked tirelessly from behind the scenes to help them rescue the innocent while also ridding the world of evil.

Only evil had won this round of life's twisted game. And if Slade and the others didn't figure out where she and her father were, they were going to lose them both forever.

"She's still alive." Apollo rumbled as he came to Slade's side. "If Reiner wanted them dead, we'd be staring at their bodies instead of an empty apartment."

He blinked as the other man's point sank deep, doing his damnedest not to let Apollo and the others see how close he was to breaking.

She's gone. They're both fucking gone!

And they had no idea where they were.

"We have to figure out where they were taken," he finally spoke his first words since arriving on scene. "We need to access the building's security cams, and—"

"I hate to be a Debbie Downer," Bones interrupted. "But isn't that the kind of stuff Shadow usually does? I mean, unless one of you guys knows how to do that sort of thing. 'Cause I sure the hell don't."

"He's right." Falcon was the next to join in on the

conversation. "None of us have the kind of technical skills required to do what's needed to find them. We need help. Big time help."

And Slade knew exactly who to call.

"Rawlins." The man's name came out as a deep grumble.

As the other men in the room started to turn his way, he was already pulling out his phone. Slade tapped the number he was damn glad that he'd saved, putting the call on speaker so everyone could hear.

The man who'd helped him when he'd first been ordered to find an MIA Shadow answered after the third ring.

"Rawlins."

"It's Garrison," Slade identified himself. "We need your help."

The man's tone was almost deadly when he responded with a curt, "Tell me."

Slade stuck to the highlights of what they knew up to that point, and then he all but begged the man when he asked, "Can you help us?"

"Help you find Owens and Shadow? I'm insulted that you thought you had to ask."

Relief filled his veins, and he wanted to reach through the phone and hug the brilliant man. But since that wasn't possible…

"We need you to hack into the security system at our current location. There are cameras in the hallway, so I'm hoping we'll get lucky and get a look at whoever it was that did this."

"Thought you already knew it was that Reiner guy."

"Oh, he's definitely involved," Bones chimed in. "But the guy's like five-five, if that. No way he got the upper hand on Owens and Shadow unless he had some help."

The sound of keys being struck at a high rate of speed filled the phone's speaker as Slade and the others waited. "Okay, I've got the feed up now. And yep, you're right. There were two assholes working together. They were dressed like fucking firefighters, if you can believe that."

"Firefighters?" Apollo frowned. "Was there a call about a fire in the building?"

A few more clicks, and Rawlins was back. "Nope. But the building security recorded two firemen being let into the building. According to the guard's notes, the firefighters claimed someone called in a possible gas leak from your location, and they'd been sent to check it out."

"Can you get facial rec?"

"Not from the camera by the apartment door, but maybe… Well hello there, Andrew Reiner. And who's that you brought with you?" The tech genius worked his magic while the men of Tac-Ops waited. "Damn. I can't make out the other guy's face enough for an ID, but you've got Reiner dead to rights. Bring him in alive, I bet he'd flip faster than an IHOP pancake during the breakfast rush."

Bones snickered, and Falcon's lips twitched with a grin, but Slade was in no mood to smile.

"Okay, so we know half of the who," he pointed out to Rawlins and his team. "But how do we figure out where?"

"You know how they found the safe house in the first place?"

"No clue."

A slight pause ensued before the man on the phone spoke up again. "Hate to ask, but any way you picked up a tail after leaving the hospital following the explosion?"

"No," Slade's response was immediate. "There's no fucking way."

"You sure?" Bones looked at him, regret filling the other man's eyes. "Don't come at me, brother, but we have to look at every possibility. Even ones that seem unlikely."

"It's not just unlikely, it didn't happen. And this isn't my ego on some big fucking trip. I'm telling you, there was no tail. You've all seen me drive whenever we're protecting total strangers. You really think I'd put Shadow at risk by not watching my rearview the entire fucking time?"

The longer he spoke, the more pissed off he became. And then he felt like shit because he knew his brothers were only trying to help. But dammit, they were wasting time asking if he'd been followed.

Time that Shadow and Rafe didn't have.

"Okay, so if you weren't followed, then how—"

"A tracker."

All eyes turned to Apollo who was staring back at Slade with a solemn expression.

"You think one of us was compromised?" He clarified, making sure he'd heard the other man correctly.

"It's the only thing that makes sense. Especially given the pictures we found at Reiner's place."

"Ooh, that's a good point." Bones nodded excitedly. "If you weren't followed, then you had to have been tracked. And since you drove the SUV from our building straight here, it couldn't have been on the car."

"It had to be on your persons," Rawlins agreed. "One of you had to have come into contact with someone you didn't know."

Digger met his teammate's stares as the answer finally began to sink in. "Shadow." He swallowed. "She was the only one checked out by the staff."

"Was there ever a time she was out of your sight?" Rawlins asked. "A time when she was alone with someone on the hospital payroll, or even another patient or visitor nearby?"

"The CT," Slade shared. "It was the only time I wasn't with her."

"Give me the name of the hospital and the time frame, and I'll see what I can find."

He recited the information for the other man as he typed. It took Rawlins less than a minute to uncover the evidence needed to prove Shadow had been unknowingly tracked.

"Oh, yeah." The man on the phone sounded hopeful as he continued to work. "Okay, so I've got Andrew Rawlins inside the E.R., and he's wearing a set of scrubs."

What the hell?

"You're sure it's him?"

"Positive. And when I go back to right when Shadow was being wheeled out of the room…bingo. Yep, there it is."

"There what is?"

"The asshole pretended to accidentally bump into the bottom corner of Shadow's gurney as the tech was wheeling her out. But when I played it in slo-mo, I caught the guy's sleight of hand. Looks like he placed something along the sole of one of her shoes."

"Which shoes?" Falcon asked next.

"White sneakers," Rawlins answered instantly. A few more clicks and then, "The same white sneakers she was wearing when the wanna-be firefighters carried her and Rafe out the floor's emergency exit."

Carried her out…

Ah, God. If they were carried out then at the very least Shadow and her father were unconscious when they were taken. Because they were hurt, or was the cause something less frightening?

Slade's gaze inadvertently slid to a spot of blood on the tiled floor.

"Rawlins, this is Falcon. Is there any way to tap into whatever system they used to track her here? If she's still wearing the shoes, there's a chance the device is still active, and if that's the case—"

"I should be able to figure out exactly where she and Owens were taken," Rawlins finished for the team's lead sniper. "It'll be tricky, and might take me a few minutes. But if I can do a quick search for any anomalistic changes in signals in or around the building at the time you arrived and compare those with the signals at the time of her and Owens' abductions…"

The man who'd already proven himself an invaluable asset took the next couple of minutes to do what he did best. Slade and his teammates waited anxiously for the results, knowing if this didn't work, they'd be back to square one.

If this doesn't work, Shadow and Rafe are both as good as dead.

But just as the gut-wrenching thought came to his mind, Rawlins renewed their hope that there might still be time. Time not only to find their teammate and boss, but to save two people they'd all come to love.

"I got her. The signal isn't great, but it will at least

get you to the building where she and Owens are being held."

The entire group of Tac-Ops operatives grew excited with visible hope.

"Where?" Slade growled, needing to get to his woman before it was too late.

"Old warehouse at the edge of NoDa." Rawlins referred to North Davidson, a neighborhood in Charlotte.

"That's like ten minutes from here," Bones exclaimed. "Max."

"Let's go." Slade spun on his heels and headed for the door.

He didn't have to look back to know his teammates were there. Because they were more than a team. They were family. And when it came to protecting their own, there wasn't anything they wouldn't do.

Minutes later, they were in the SUV and racing to the woman Slade loved. Rather than get behind the wheel, he let Apollo drive while he focused on his phone.

With the warehouse's address programmed into the vehicle's GPS, and his fellow SEAL brother at the helm, Slade focused on the phone still held tightly in his hand as he studied the blueprints Rawlins sent just before they'd left.

The abandoned warehouse was large, and at first he felt defeated. But then he forced the emotion he was feeling aside and called upon his training. Once that happened, it didn't take long for him to deduce the best, safest way for him and his team to enter the building.

"We'll enter through the north." He spoke loud enough so that his teammates and Rawlins could hear. "There's a door there we should be able to breach."

"You bring the goods?" Bones asked, presumably referring to his go-to breaching device.

"No." Slade shook his head. "Not unless we've got one in here."

They hadn't taken the time to stop and load up on weapons. None of them wore any sort of protective vest or gear.

"Looks like we're going old-school, boys." Bones didn't sound the least bit disappointed.

Slade just prayed it would be enough.

The drive that should have taken ten took six, thanks to Apollo's expert moves behind the wheel. There wasn't time for as much stealth as they normally would have used. But they did leave the car's doors open to help with what noise control they could.

The soles of their boots ground against worn asphalt and weeds. Slade was first at the door, and he didn't wait to reach for the round, rusty knob. To his surprise, it turned with relative ease.

With a single pull, the door opened fully. Slade covered up top, while Apollo crouched down to cover low.

Falcon and Bones entered first, their pistols up and at the ready. Apollo went next, followed immediately by Slade. And when the entire team was in, they stopped to regroup.

Before exiting the SUV, Slade had put an earbud in his left ear and slid his phone into the back pocket of his jeans. Rawlins was still on the phone, taking Shadow's place as the team's overwatch. And though he'd give anything to hear her voice, Slade was damn glad the other man was there.

"The signal's still showing strong in the northeast corner of the building," the deep voice in his ear sounded. "You should see a hallway due east and to your right."

Slade turned that way, looking through the low-lit space. Past a large, concrete pillar he saw nothing at first but a darkened corner.

"You see it?"

Not yet.

He took a few steps closer in that direction. Not far, but enough to give him a better view.

"I see it," Slade whispered back, using hand movements to signal to the team they should move.

Just as they had on the countless missions before, the four men moved as one past the giant pillar and beyond. When they reached the hallway's edge, Slade swung his weapon around the corner in case there were any threats.

But there was nothing but more shadows and the

occasional ray of light that shone in from opened doorways along the narrow space. What that told him was that there were several rooms needing to be cleared.

Pulling in a deep breath, he let it out slowly, and with his weapon at the ready, he motioned to his men. Slade took the lead with the others in line behind him. Apollo's hand was on Slade's left shoulder, while Bones' hand was on Apollo's. Falcon brought up the rear, his hand on Bones' shoulder.

Together, they quickly began clearing the rooms.

The first one was empty, as were the second and third. Slade tried like hell not to think about how long this section of the building was, or how many rooms they'd have to check before finding the only one they needed.

At least eight that I can see. Maybe more.

He pushed the useless thoughts away and took a step toward the next doorway. He swung his weapon inside and then—

Bang!

His heart stopped as he and the others recognized the sound for exactly what it was. Someone had just shot a fucking gun, and it had come from somewhere down the hall.

Shadow!

Slade took off in a dead sprint, no longer giving a damn about being quiet. The others followed with a pace matching his own.

From a room several yards away, he could hear what sounded like a loud, almost animalistic growl. His heart thundered inside his chest as he willed his legs and feet to move faster than ever before. When they got to the room where Shadow and her father were being held, the scene before him left his heart filled with a combination of relief, fury, and overwhelming dread.

She's alive!

Slade wanted to bawl like a damn baby when he saw Shadow standing on her own two feet. Then he wanted to find the son of a bitch who'd beat her with what looked to be an inch of her life.

Her hands and forearms were covered in blood, but when he saw the man lying on the floor behind her, he understood why.

No!

Owens was on his back a few feet from Shadow. His eyes were closed, and the front of his shirt was soaked with the man's blood.

It was obvious he'd been shot, but the slight rising and falling of his chest was a good sign. He was alive, at least.

For now.

Slade's gaze went back to Shadow, who had yet to see him. She was too busy holding a knife toward the man behind her and her father's abductions.

Michael Stanton stood facing her from a few feet

away. His face was bloody, and it was obvious his nose had been broken.

"On your knees, Stanton," Slade ordered, despite the urge to pull his own trigger.

The world would be a much better place without the son of a bitch in it.

At the sound of his voice, Shadow blinked and turned his way. The emotion he saw there nearly dropped him to his knees.

"Slade?"

"Yeah, princess. It's me." He gave her a curt nod to let her know she was going to be okay.

Those were the same words he'd given to her that night in the motel, and then again at the cabin when she'd woken from a very bad dream.

The star of that nightmare had been the man slowly bringing himself to his knees. But it was over. Stanton was finished, and he would never hurt anyone else ever—

"Wait." Shadow came to his side. She reached up and took the gun from his hand.

With Bones and Falcon giving medical aid to Owens, Apollo stood close by while Slade willingly surrendered his weapon.

He watched carefully as she lifted the pistol, pointing its barrel in the dead center of Stanton's head.

"He killed my mother while she slept." Her voice sounded small, almost childlike. To Stanton, she said,

"You were her partner. You were supposed to be her *friend.*"

"She was going to t-turn me in." Stanton began stuttering like the chickenshit that he was. "Y-Your mother grew soft. *You* m-made her soft."

"No!" Shadow took a broad step toward him. "You do *not* get to put my mother's death…my mother's murder…on me. *You* did this. All of it. This is all on *you!*"

"I only did what I had to. I was just trying to survive!"

"Bullshit." Shadow's voice returned to a slow, lethal tone. "The choices you made weren't out of necessity. They came from greed and your own cowardice. And look at where it got you." She laughed humorlessly as she glanced around the room.

"You think I'm the only person in the CIA to ever use their contacts and skills to their own advantage? I'm not!" Spittle flew from Stanton's mouth.

"I don't care about any other dirty agents, asshole." Shadow shook her head slowly. "Frankly, I don't even care about you. You're a traitor to your country. For that alone, you deserve to die. But for the cold-blooded murder of my mother…a woman who trusted you to have her back…a woman who brought you into her home…for that, you deserve to suffer."

"Suffer?" The idiot huffed out another sardonic breath. "Please. You're not going to shoot me. You're soft, like your mother. You don't have the ba—"

Shadow pulled the trigger, the deafening sound making him and every man on his team jump from the unexpected blast. Stanton howled in pain, his left hand grabbing hold of his right.

His dominant hand. His shooting hand. And from the looks of it, a hand the asshole would never use again.

Slade looked to Shadow who turned and handed him back his gun. If he wasn't already in love with the incredible woman, that would have done it right there.

"Feel better?" He couldn't help but flash her a grin.

He expected a nod, or a teeny tiny smile. But the strongest woman he'd ever met gave a slow shake of her head as a river of tears poured from her eyes.

"Ah, baby." Slade pulled her into his arms but let go when she gasped in pain. "What is it?" he looked down at her, trying to figure out where else she'd been hurt.

"My ribs." She put a hand to her side right side, clearly having trouble pulling in a full, deep breath. "Pretty sure at least one of my ribs are broken."

Son of a…

"Uh…Digger?" Rawlins' voice sounded in Slade's ear.

Shit. "I'm here."

"What do you need?"

"Three ambulances," Slade answered without

hesitation. "Owens is alive, but he took one to the gut."

"Three?" Rawlins paused. "I thought I heard two gunshots."

"You did," Slade confirmed. "Stanton shot Owens, and then Shadow shot Stanton."

"Holy shit. He dead?"

"Unfortunately, no. But I don't think he'll be shaking many hands on the campaign trail anytime soon."

And from the look on the pathetic man's face, even the disgraced senator knew that his time in politics—and as a free man—had just come to an end.

"Atta girl." The other man sounded pleased. "Who needs the third ride?"

Slade turned to the woman who was clearly overrun with shock. "Shadow."

"She hit?"

"No, but she took one hell of a beating." To her, he had to know, "Did Stanton do that?"

"He hit me once." She nodded. "But the rest was from one of the two guys who broke into the apartment and took us."

"One was Reiner," Slade informed her. "Not sure about the other yet. But don't worry," Slade vowed. "We'll get them both."

And anyone else involved in Stanton's fucked up plan.

"Police and ambulance are on their way," Rawlins let him know in a rush.

Relaying the info to the team, Slade told the others, "Cops and medical are on their way."

With that handled, his focus returned to the woman next to him. She was still in shock and shaking like a damn leaf.

While Apollo used some plastic ties he'd had in the car to secure Stanton, who was still writhing in pain, Slade helped Shadow walk back over to her dad.

"H-How b-bad?" she asked for her father's prognosis.

"He's lost a lot of blood," Bones stated the obvious. "But I think he's going to be okay. It's impossible to know for sure until the medics get him to the hospital, but from what I can see, it doesn't look like the bullet hit anything vital."

"Oh, thank God."

Shadow nearly collapsed in relief, but Slade was right there, more than ready to catch her.

"I love you, Alice," he whispered in her ear as he held her in his arms with kid gloves.

She leaned back just enough that her watery blue eyes could meet his. "What did you just say?"

Her widened gaze was filled with shock, but this time it had nothing to do with the horrors she'd faced.

"I said I love you. And I hope like hell you can somehow find a way to love me back."

"I don't have to find a way, Slade." She reached up and cupped one side of his face. "Because I already do."

"Say it." He knew they were being watched and didn't care. "I need to hear the words."

"I love you, too, Slade Matthew Garrison. I'm pretty sure a part of me always has."

"Awwww…" Rawlin's voice interrupted the most precious moment of his life.

Reaching up, Slade removed the earbud from his ear. And then, with the lightest of kisses to keep from hurting her, he leaned in and pressed his lips to hers.

EPILOGUE

Rafe Owens' plantation
Somewhere near Charlotte

Three months later…

"Seriously, Alice." Evie Mitchell, Bones' fiancée, shook her head in awe. "It might be small, but this is one of the most beautiful weddings I've ever been to."

Shadow…no, *Alice*…was still getting used to hearing people call her by her real name. She'd answer to either, of course. But today of all days, it was good to simply be…

"Alice Garrison." Nicki McAllister toyed with the sound of the name. "It does have a nice ring to it. Speaking of rings…" Apollo's wife reached out and lifted Alice's left hand. "I have to hand it to Dig, the man does have good taste."

"Of course, I do." Her husband sidled up beside her.

With his hand around her beaded waist, Slade leaned in and pressed his lips to the top of her veiled head.

"Hey, you." She looked up at the most handsome man to have ever put on a tux.

"Hey, yourself." He went in for a more proper kiss.

The women around them all began to croon.

"Awwww..." The group of Tac-Ops wives gave a collective sigh.

Falcon's wife was next in line to chime in.

"I'll admit," Avery Morgan gave the happy couple a big, toothy smile. "I never thought I'd see the day when Slade Garrison would say 'I do'."

"You and me, both," Alice wrapped an arm around her husband.

Man, she really liked how that sounded.

A popular song began to play, and the other women began grabbing each other to dance. But she stayed right where she was, because there was nowhere else she'd rather be. Except maybe in the honeymoon suite at the hotel where they planned to spend the night.

"Rawlins called," Slade told her. "Said he was

sorry he couldn't make it, but to make sure you knew there was a gift on the way."

"Oh, no." Alice chuckled. "Should we be scared?"

"With that man? You never can tell."

No, you definitely couldn't. But something told her whatever Baker Rawlins had purchased would be something the two of them could put to good use.

Alice was so thankful for the man and his willingness to step in to help the team. If not for him, she and her father would both be dead. And Michael Stanton and his cronies would still be roaming free.

Thankfully, that wasn't the case.

Stanton's lawyer managed to get him a deal designed specifically to avoid the death penalty. With what he'd confessed—and a team of highly trained agents who were truly loyal to their country—there was enough evidence against him to all but guarantee a conviction.

She knew this. The former senator knew this. And apparently, his lawyer did, too.

It's why Stanton was quick to give up Andrew Reiner and Doug Easton as the two men who helped in the attempted murders of her and her father. Both Reiner and Easton also pled guilty, which allowed everyone involved to avoid a lengthy and emotional trial.

Alice's blue gaze slid across the large ballroom to where her father and Falcon's brother stood talking.

The expression on Coulter Morgan's face looked serious, as did her father's.

Her gut tightened a bit because, whatever they were discussing, it didn't look good. And given she knew the truth about Colt's job…

"I'll give you a penny for your thoughts."

She looked up to see Slade's breathtaking smile, loving that it was all for her. "I was just thinking what a lucky girl I am."

"Liar." He nudged her with a knowing grin.

"That's not a lie." She shook her head with an adamant, "That's not a lie. I *am* lucky."

More so than she had the right to be.

"Oh, I know you are." Her husband teased. "But that's not what you were thinking."

Damn. She forgot for a moment how good he was at reading her face.

"You know, this was a whole lot easier when I was just a voice in your ear."

"Maybe." He pulled her body flush with his and leaned in. "But being face-to-face…" His lips feathered over hers in a barely there kiss. "Is a hell of a lot more fun."

Alice threw her head back and laughed. "That it is, Mr. Garrison. That, it is."

"You gonna tell me what you were thinking?"

"Man, you are like a dog with a bone, you know that?" She gave in when he simply smiled back at her with an expectantly arched brow. "Okay, fine. I was watching my father and Colt talk." She motioned to where the two men were still standing across the room. "Not sure what's going on, but it looks pretty serious."

And yeah, after nearly losing her father to Stanton's bullet, she'd turned into an overprotective daughter.

So sue me.

"Well, it *is* Coulter Morgan," Slade grinned. "The guy's probably trying to talk your dad into investing in his latest get-rich-quick scheme."

Alice chuckled, but inside her stomach grew tight. Because there was a lot more to Coulter Morgan than Slade or the other members of Tac-Ops knew.

And if the truth were to ever come out…

"Let's go." She reached down and grabbed Slade's strong hand. "Let's say our goodbyes and then blow this joint."

"In a hurry to start the honeymoon, Mrs. Garrison?" He allowed her to pull him along.

Alice stopped mid-stride to turn back around, sending the man of her dreams another smile. "No." She shook her head as she rose onto her tiptoes to give him a kiss. "I mean, of course, I am, but it's more than that."

"Yeah?"

She nodded and placed a palm on his suited chest. "I'm in a hurry to start this new life that we've been blessed with. To wake up to this face as many mornings as possible. To fall asleep in these arms every night that you're home."

"And when I'm not home?"

"I'll be in your ear, ready to have your back. Just like you had mine."

Slade's gaze became glossy, and for a moment she thought for sure the man was going to cry. Instead, he leaned down, taking her by complete surprise when he scooped her off her feet.

"Slade!"

"Fuck the goodbyes." He spun them around and began marching toward the room's nearest exit. "We'll see them all again soon enough."

Alice laughed even as she tried arguing that they couldn't leave. "We can't just—"

"It's our wedding, princess. We can do whatever the hell we want."

She glanced back from over his shoulder at the small crowd. They were laughing and talking. Dancing and singing. Even her father wasn't paying any attention to the fact that they were walking away.

A smile spread across her face, deciding Slade was right. This was the perfect time for their departure. And the sooner she and Slade checked into their honeymoon suite downtown…

She grabbed the side of his rugged face and brought his mouth to hers. His steps faltered, but he never came close to letting her go.

He'll never let me fall.

Those words were true in both their literal and figurative forms. And as he broke away from the kiss to look down into her eyes, she knew her life had truly begun.

"I love you, Alice. Or Shadow. Or whatever other name you want me to call you."

"Yours." She stared back at her future. "I just want you to call me yours."

* * *

One week later…

Coulter Morgan looked both ways before he crossed the street. As he walked toward the art gallery's entrance, he gave his surroundings a quick, assessing glance. Tonight was the night shit was going to come together, and he couldn't wait for it to be over.

After months of planning, surveilling—and endless conversations with the pretentious assholes he's just as soon shoot than see again—he was finally going to get his meet-and-greet with the man his agency has been after for years.

He glanced down at the overpriced watch he'd been given specifically for this occasion. Like his designer suit and tie…and hell, even his uncomfortable as shit shoes…the watch was a prop to help pull off the dangerous one-man show.

The role he was playing was the same one he'd been performing for the past several weeks. A rich, entitled, American heir willing to spend millions on his own personal sex slave.

Cases like this were the absolute worst. Their targets the sickest of the sick. Twisted freaks who got their rocks off by forcing themselves onto the woman they'd kidnapped and, oftentimes, beaten.

That was the very sort of man Coulter was on his way to meet. The kind of man he himself had been pretending to be.

I can't wait to rid the world of this sick son of a bitch.

He stepped up to the guarded door, toward the well-dressed man standing guard. The very large, very serious-looking man stared him up and down.

"Good evening." Coulter flashed the man his best rich man smile.

"Invitation." The man grumbled.

Apparently, that was the only greeting he'd receive.

"Of course." He pulled out the fancy envelope he'd talked his way into receiving.

The massive wall of muscle studied the invite more carefully than one would normally expect.

Coulter was ready for the close inspection, however, because he knew what tonight was really about. This wasn't simply an innocent gathering of appreciation for the showcased artist's craft, but rather a meeting of the rich and twisted designed for the gallery's real reason for existing.

The bouncer returned the thick cardstock and opened the door. As Coulter stepped inside, he wondered if the icy reception was because the other man disapproved of his boss's underhanded dealings, or if the big guy showed the same sunny disposition to everyone who crossed his path.

Can't blame the guy for thinking I'm a disgusting pig. I feel like one, and I'm only pretending.

How these so-called men lived with themselves, he'd never know. Which was why he had been working so damn hard to weasel his way into their nauseating circle.

Coulter glanced around, doing his best to fit in with the uber rich crowd. He could practically smell the money rolling off these perverts' backs, and he couldn't wait to be done with this job so he could finally move onto the next.

"Champagne?"

A young woman appeared suddenly by his side. She was dressed in a scrap of black lace that barely covered, well, anything. Balanced in her hand was a large, round tray topped with several filled-to-the-brim crystal flutes.

"Thank you." Coulter selected the nearest flute, giving the youthful server a nod and a smile.

His chest tightened as she walked away, his eyes

following her every move. Though it was impossible to know for sure, he prayed like hell she wasn't one of the girls being auctioned off soon.

"She's a little young for you, isn't she, Colt?"

Every muscle beneath his designer suit froze. That voice. He *knew* that voice. Only…

No, no, no, no, no. It can't be her. She isn't supposed to be here.

He'd personally seen the names of those who'd been given invitations, and this woman was *not* on that list. But as he slid his gaze to the woman standing at his left, Coulter's fears were brought to fruition.

Son of a…

"Alex?" He hurriedly glanced around before looking back at Falcon's sister-in-law.

Alexandria Webb was the bane of his very existence. Mainly because the gorgeous brunette starred in the best of his dreams while in reality, well…

The stunning woman would barely give him the time of day.

"What are you doing here?" He demanded a bit more harshly than was his intent.

"Wow." She blinked those big brown eyes of hers. "Good to see you, too. And I was about to ask you the same thing. Because, well, the thing is…*I'm* an artist."

"So?"

"So it makes sense for me to be here. You know, at an art gallery? But you—"

"You have to leave," he cut her off sharply. "Now."

Alex blinked again, her dark brows dipping low with confusion. "Excuse me?"

"I'm serious, Alex. This place…" He looked around again. "You don't want anything to do with these people. Trust me on this."

"Okay, first of all, I'm not sure how *you* got invited to tonight's showing. But *I* was given a personal invitation by the gallery owner himself."

The twisting Coulter felt in his gut the second he'd seen her gorgeous face worsened. "Gordon Crawford personally asked you to come here?"

"You don't have to sound so surprised. I do own my own successful gallery, you know. Albeit on a much smaller scale. But yes, Mr. Crawford stumbled upon my place last week. Apparently, he liked what he saw and gave me an invitation on the spot."

Liked what he saw. I just bet the bastard liked what he saw.

Long legs. Straight, dark hair that was cut in a sharp angle at her delicate jaw. Eyes Coulter could get lost in if she'd let him, and a set of full, ruby red lips he wished like hell he could taste.

In fact, when it came to this woman, there wasn't a single thing he didn't like. Even her feisty, stay-away-from-me attitude where he was concerned was a giant freaking turn-on.

I'm pathetic, I know. But hey, at least I own that shit.

As for Alex being here by way of Crawford's personal invitation…this was bad. Like really, really bad.

"Alex, listen to me." He pleaded with her. "I promise I'll explain everything later. But right now, I really need you to—"

"Mr. Morris!" A commanding voice boomed over the low humming of the well-dressed crowd.

Of. Fucking. Course.

Coulter looked away from Alex's stare to see the man of the hour weaving his way through the dense crowd. Luckily, he was stopping and shaking hands with those he'd thought worthy enough to allow here, which would probably buy him an extra minute or two…at best.

He locked gazes with Crawford from across the room. The man eyed him closely, and even from here it was clear he'd taken notice in the familiar way Coulter and Alex were conversing.

Think, Coulter. Think!

If Alex blew this for him, they would both end up dead. And as the powerful man made his way closer, there was only one plausible idea racing through his head.

He slid his beseeching gaze back to Alex, who was still looking at him as if he'd grown two heads. "I promise, I'll explain everything later," he repeated. "But for the sake of both of our lives, I need you to play along."

"Play along?" She frowned again. "With what?"

They were running out of time, and he knew what had to be done. She'd hate it. Might even slap him into next week. Either way, he was damn good at improvisation. So he was ready for whatever reaction the spunky woman decided to give.

Praying the plan he'd come up with wouldn't end with Crawford signing their death warrants, Coulter leaned in close and cupped her cheeks with both of his hands.

"Colt, what are you—"

"For the rest of tonight, my name is Cole Morris. And I'm not your sister's brother-in-law…I'm your date."

"You're my what?"

"Here he comes. I'm serious, Alex. If you blow my cover, we'll both wind up dead."

"Your cover?"

"Please, Alexandria. Do us both a giant favor, and just…play along."

He pulled back to look into her mesmerizing stare. Alex opened her luscious mouth, most likely to search for more answers he couldn't give.

But rather than attempt another half-assed explanation, Coulter held her flawless face in his hands, and then…

He kissed her.

ALSO BY ANNA BLAKELY

Check it out! Anna Blakely has three new series:

TAC-OPS Series

Garrett's Destiny

Ethan's Obsession

Beckett's Desire

Slade's Vow

Marked Series

Marked For Death

Marked for Revenge

Marked for Deception

Marked for Obsession

Marked for Danger

Marked for Disaster

Marked for Vengeance

Charlie Team

(R.I.S.C. Spinoff Series)

Kellan

Asher

Greyson

Rhys

Other Books by Anna

Eagle's Nest Securities Series

Keeping His Promise

Playing With Fire

Flirting With Danger

Protecting His Future

Forgiving His Past

R.I.S.C. Series (Alpha Team)

Taking a Risk, Part One

Taking a Risk, Part Two

Beautiful Risk

Intentional Risk

Unpredictable Risk

Ultimate Risk

Targeted Risk

Savage Risk

Undeniable Risk

His Greatest Risk

Bravo Team Series

Rescuing Gracelynn (Nate & Gracie)

Rescuing Katherine (Matt & Katherine)

Rescuing Gabriella (Zade & Gabby)

Rescuing Ellena (Gabe & Elle)

Rescuing Jenna (Adrian & Jenna)

R.I.S.C. Charlie Team Series

Kellan

Greyson

Asher

Rhys

Parker

R.I.S.C. Delta Team Series

Christian

Brody

John

ABOUT THE AUTHOR

Author Anna Blakely brings you stories of love, action, and edge-of-your-seat suspense. As an avid reader of romantic suspense herself, Anna's dream is to create stories her readers will enjoy and characters they'll fall in love with as much as she has. She believes in true love and happily-ever-after, and that's what she will always bring to you.

Anna lives in rural Missouri with her husband, children, and several rescued animals. When she's not writing, Anna enjoys reading, watching action and horror movies (the scarier the better), and spending time with her amazing husband, four wonderful children, and her adorable granddaughter.

FB Author Page: facebook.com/annablakely.author.7
Blakely's Bunch (reader group): https://www.facebook.com/groups/354218335396441/
Instagram: https://instagram.com/annablakely
BookBub: https//www.bookbub.com/authors/anna-blakely
Amazon: amazon.com/author/annablakely

Twitter: @ablakelyauthor

Goodreads: https://www.goodreads.com/author/show/18650841.Anna_Blakely

facebook.com/annablakely.author.7

x.com/ablakelyauthor

instagram.com/annablakely

amazon.com/author/annablakely

There are many more books in this fan fiction world than listed here, for an up-to-date list go to www.AcesPress.com

You can also visit our Amazon page at: http://www.amazon.com/author/operationalpha

Special Forces: Operation Alpha World

Christie Adams: Charity's Heart
Elizabella Baker: Challenging Luke
Linzi Baxter: Dangerous Rescue
Misha Blake: Flash
Anna Blakely: Rescuing Gracelynn
Julia Bright: Saving Lorelei
Cara Carnes: Protecting Mari
Kendra Mei Chailyn: Beast
Melissa Kay Clarke: Rescuing Annabeth
Gia Cobie: Saved from Revenge
Samantha Cole: Handling Haven
Cassie Colton: Rescuing Ryder
KaLyn Cooper: Spring Unveiled
Jordan Dane: Redemption for Avery
D.M. Earl: Claire's Guardian
Riley Edwards: Protecting Olivia
Dorothy Ewels: Knight's Queen
Lila Ferrari: Protecting Joy
Nicole Flockton: Protecting Maria
Lea Griffith: Finding Ava
Desiree Holt: Protecting Maddie

Bree Hera: Trusting the Team
Rayne Lewis: Justice for Mary
Kristin Lynn: Worth the Risk
JM Madden: Rescuing Olivia
A.M. Mahler: Griffin
Ellie Masters: Sybil's Protector
Trish McCallan: Hero Under Fire
Naomi McKay: Twist
KD Michaels: Saving Laura
Olivia Michaels: Protecting Harper
Annie Miller: Securing Willow
MJ Nightingale: Protecting Beauty
C.K. O'Connor: Delaney's Bodyguard
Danielle Pays: Defending Sarina
Lainey Reese: Protecting New York
Taryn Rivers: Savage Cove
TL Reeve and Michele Ryan: Extracting Mateo
Ariana Rose: Chasing Paige
Angela Rush: Charlotte
E.M. Shue: Discovering Tyler
Heather Slade: Code Name: Admiral
Dee Stewart: Fighting for Brielle
Lynne St. James: SEAL's Spitfire
Bella Stone: Rexar
Jen Talty: Protecting Ainsley
Reina Torres, Rescuing Hi'ilani
LJ Vickery: Circus Comes to Town
R. C. Wynne: Shadows Renewed
Amanda Zook: Freeing Camila

Delta Team Three Series

Lori Ryan: Nori's Delta
Becca Jameson: Destiny's Delta
Lynne St James, Gwen's Delta
Elle James: Ivy's Delta
Riley Edwards: Hope's Delta

Police and Fire: Operation Alpha World

Freya Barker: Burning for Autumn
B.P. Beth: Scott
Jane Blythe: Salvaging Marigold
Julia Bright: Justice for Amber
Gia Cobie: Saved from Revenge
Leyna Cohan: Embracing Juliette
Nicole Craig: Justice for Francesca
Danielle M. Haas: Crossroads of Betrayal
Deanndra Hall: Shelter for Sharla
India Kells: Game Master
Reina Torres: Justice for Sloane

Tarpley VFD Series

Silver James, Fighting for Elena
Deanndra Hall, Fighting for Carly
Haven Rose, Fighting for Calliope
MJ Nightingale, Fighting for Jemma
TL Reeve, Fighting for Brittney
Nicole Flockton, Fighting for Nadia

As you know, this book included at least one character from Susan Stoker's books. To check out more, see below.

SEAL of Protection: Alliance Series

Protecting Remi
Protecting Wren
Protecting Josie
Protecting Maggie
Protecting Addison
Protecting Kelli (Sept 2, 2025)
Protecting Bree (Jan 6, 2026)

Rescue Angels Series

Keeping Laryn (July 1, 2025)
Keeping Amanda (Nov 4, 2025)
Keeping Zita (Feb 10, 2026)
Keeping Penny (TBA)
Keeping Kara (TBA)
Keeping Jennifer (TBA)

The Refuge Series

Deserving Alaska
Deserving Henley
Deserving Reese
Deserving Cora
Deserving Lara
Deserving Maisy

Deserving Ryleigh

SEAL Team Hawaii Series

Finding Elodie
Finding Lexie
Finding Kenna
Finding Monica
Finding Carly
Finding Ashlyn
Finding Jodelle

Eagle Point Search & Rescue

Searching for Lilly
Searching for Elsie
Searching for Bristol
Searching for Caryn
Searching for Finley
Searching for Heather
Searching for Khloe

Delta Team Two Series

Shielding Gillian
Shielding Kinley
Shielding Aspen
Shielding Jayme (novella)
Shielding Riley
Shielding Devyn
Shielding Ember
Shielding Sierra

SEAL of Protection: Legacy Series

Securing Caite (FREE!)
Securing Brenae (novella)
Securing Sidney
Securing Piper
Securing Zoey
Securing Avery
Securing Kalee
Securing Jane

Delta Force Heroes Series

Rescuing Rayne
Rescuing Aimee (novella)
Rescuing Emily
Rescuing Harley
Marrying Emily (novella)
Rescuing Kassie
Rescuing Bryn
Rescuing Casey
Rescuing Sadie (novella)
Rescuing Wendy
Rescuing Mary
Rescuing Macie (novella)
Rescuing Annie

Badge of Honor: Texas Heroes Series

Justice for Mackenzie (FREE!)
Justice for Mickie
Justice for Corrie

Justice for Laine (novella)
Shelter for Elizabeth
Justice for Boone
Shelter for Adeline
Shelter for Sophie
Justice for Erin
Justice for Milena
Shelter for Blythe
Justice for Hope
Shelter for Quinn
Shelter for Koren
Shelter for Penelope

SEAL of Protection Series

Protecting Caroline (FREE!)
Protecting Alabama
Protecting Fiona
Marrying Caroline (novella)
Protecting Summer
Protecting Cheyenne
Protecting Jessyka
Protecting Julie (novella)
Protecting Melody
Protecting the Future
Protecting Kiera (novella)
Protecting Alabama's Kids (novella)
Protecting Dakota
Protecting Tex

New York Times, *USA Today* and *Wall Street Journal* Bestselling Author Susan Stoker has a heart as big as the state of Tennessee where she lives, but this all American girl has also spent the last fourteen years living in Missouri, California, Colorado, Indiana, and Texas. She's married to a retired Army man who now gets to follow *her* around the country.

www.stokeraces.com
www.AcesPress.com
susan@stokeraces.com

Made in United States
Orlando, FL
29 November 2025